—— 圖解基礎技法・掌握素描訣竅 ——

鉛筆素描

〈中英對照解說〉

Introduction
to Pencil Drawing

鍾江村——譯

東京武藏野美術學院
製作

笛藤出版

—— 圖解基礎技法‧掌握素描訣竅 ——

〈中英對照解說〉

鉛筆素描
Introduction to Pencil Drawing

鉛筆素描：圖解基礎技法.掌握素描訣竅/東京武藏野美術學院著；
鍾江村譯. -- 3版. -- 臺北市：笛藤出版, 2021.12
面； 公分
ISBN 978-957-710-841-8(平裝)

1.鉛筆畫 2.素描 3.繪畫技法

948.2   110019616

2024年5月10日 3版第2刷 定價340元

著者	東京武藏野美術學院
譯者	鍾江村
編輯	羅巧儀
封面設計	王舒玗
總編輯	賴巧凌
編輯企劃	笛藤出版
發行所	八方出版股份有限公司
發行人	林建仲
地址	台北市中山區長安東路二段171號3樓3室
電話	(02) 2777-3682
傳真	(02) 2777-3672
總經銷	聯合發行股份有限公司
地址	新北市新店區寶橋路235巷6弄6號2樓
電話	(02)2917-8022‧(02)2917-8042
製版廠	造極彩色印刷製版股份有限公司
地址	新北市中和區中山路2段380巷7號1樓
電話	(02)2240-0333‧(02)2248-3904
印刷廠	皇甫彩藝印刷股份有限公司
地址	新北市中和區中正路988巷10號
電話	(02) 3234-5871
郵撥帳戶	八方出版股份有限公司
郵撥帳號	19809050

CULTURE SERIES ENPITSU DESIGN
©HIDEO YAMAUCHI 1991
Originally published in Japan in 1991 by GRAPHIC-SHA PUBLISHING CO.,LTD
Chinese translation rights arranged through
TOHAN CORPORATION, TOKYO.

目　次　Contents

原寸大素描（書後附圖）解說
　　要凸顯花和花邊的白色，選擇黑色調的花瓶和濃色調的椅子。可忽略背景中花邊布的模樣，使用比實際稍暗的調子處理，這樣就能夠凸顯主題的白花（用B3素描紙，用B，4B鉛筆）。

Explanation of Actual Size Drawing (Enclosed in rear of book)
In order to make the white flowers and lace stand out, I chose a dark vase and a chair with dark tones. By blurring the detail of the lace in the background and shading it darker than it really is, it is possible to make the flowers stand out more (B3 drawing paper, B 4B pencils used)

前　言

　　本書是以鉛筆做畫材，學習繪畫最基礎的表現——素描——而寫的，並以圖解及參考例子，附上解說使讀者一看即會。本書各章節的內容從鉛筆的使用方法、理解物體的結構、表現明暗及質感等基礎知識加以解說，再加上各個不同對象的表現如靜物、人物、風景等，並以具體的圖解及參考例子來解說。

　　對有志成爲畫家、插畫家、設計者而言，素描是最基本的實力，希望本書能爲你們紮下基礎並熟練各種技法。

Prologue

This book was written in order to explain the basics of pencil drawing through the use of examples and hints that make it extremely easy to understand. It starts by explaining how to use a pencil then moves on through the understanding the subject to shading and expression of depth, explaining all the techniques involved with each stage. It shows how to draw still-life, portraits and scenery, each step having examples and explanations that make the meaning self-evident. Sketching is a vital technique for anyone aiming to become a painter, illustrator or designer and I hope that this book will allow you to thoroughly master the various techniques.

第 1 章
鉛筆的使用法

Chapter 1

Pencil Techniqes

鉛筆的軟硬
Hard and Soft Pencils

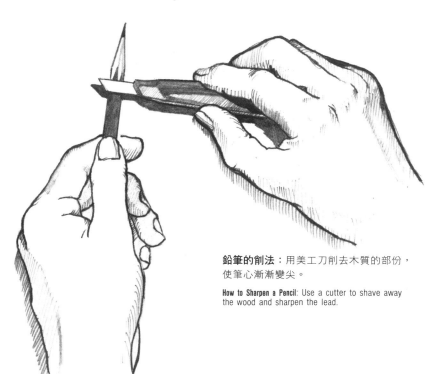

鉛筆的削法：用美工刀削去木質的部份，使筆心漸漸變尖。

How to Sharpen a Pencil: Use a cutter to shave away the wood and sharpen the lead.

削好的鉛筆

A properly sharpened pencil.

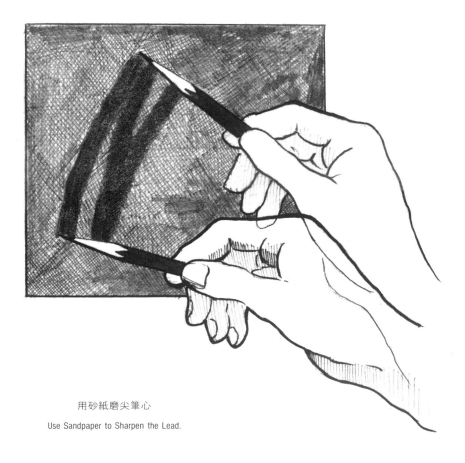

用砂紙磨尖筆心

Use Sandpaper to Sharpen the Lead.

在鉛筆素描時，可準備3～4種不同硬度的筆心。一般從4H到H為硬鉛筆，2B到6B為軟鉛筆。還有F和HB，B為中硬度的鉛筆。愈軟的鉛筆愈黑，也愈容易擦掉。

Before starting a drawing, three or four pencils of varying hardness should be readied. '4H' to 'H' are classed as hard, '2B' to '6B' are classed as soft and 'F', 'HB' and 'B' are classed as medium. The softer the pencil, the blacker the line it produces and the quicker it wears out.

硬鉛筆

Hard Pencils.

中硬度鉛筆

Medium Pencils.

軟鉛筆

Soft Pencils.

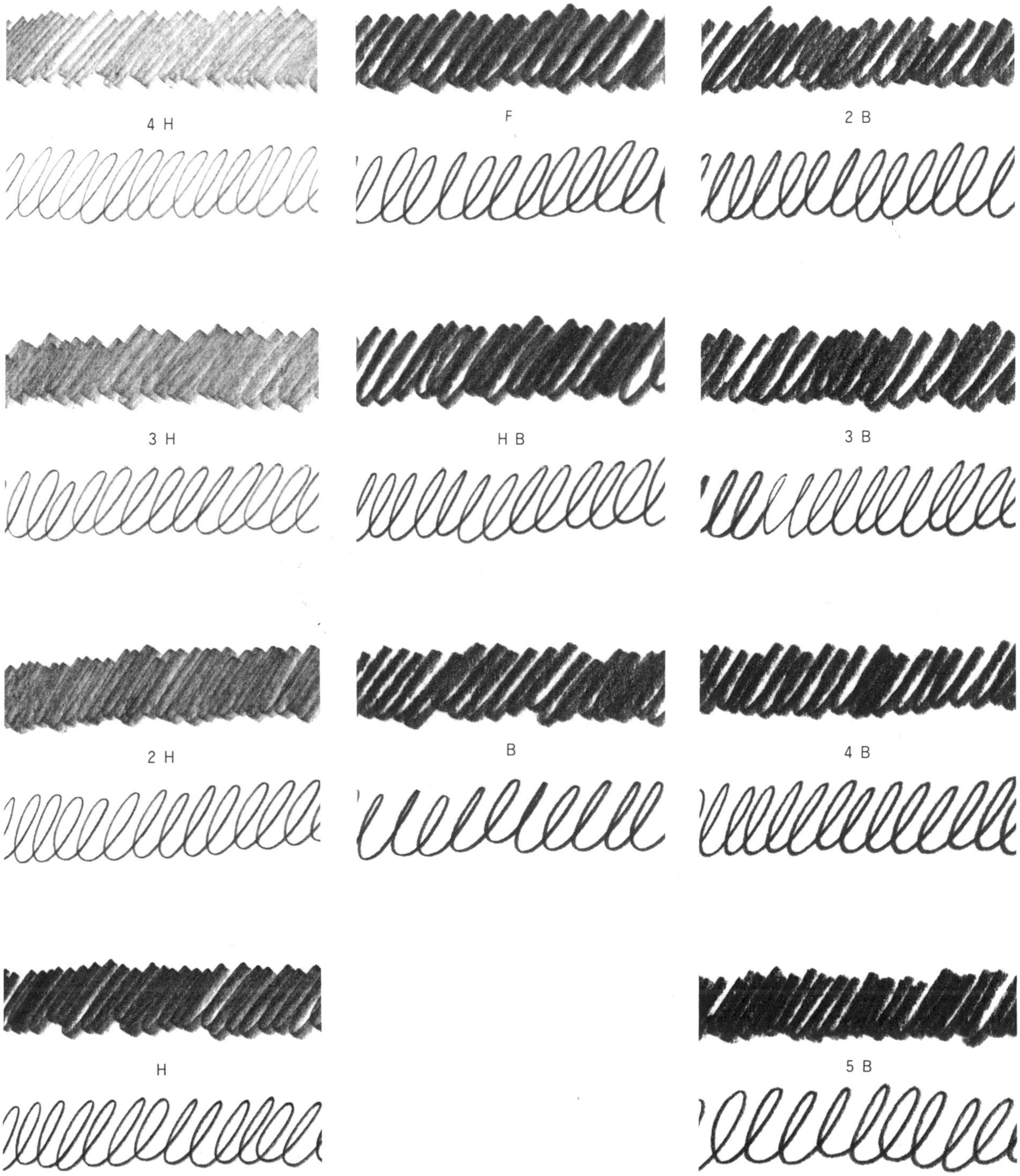

4 H

F

2 B

3 H

H B

3 B

2 H

B

4 B

H

5 B

鉛筆和線
Pencils and Lines

同樣的一支鉛筆可依繪畫的速度、筆壓的強弱、持筆的方式不同,而表現出各種不同的線條。可和沾水筆一樣,從尖細到粗軟都可表現,以線條重疊的方法,可表現出明暗,是非常方便的畫材。用橡皮擦和紙筆併用、巧妙地使用軟筆或硬筆,更能擴大素描的表現,希望你能找到適合自己的技法。

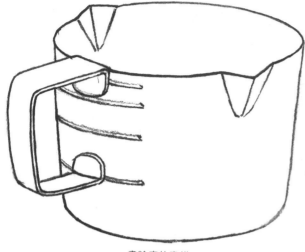

畫輪廓的素描

A sketch of the outline.

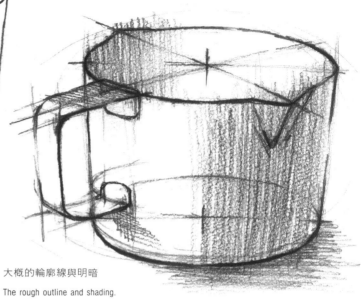

大概的輪廓線與明暗

The rough outline and shading.

1支鉛筆可作多種線條表現。

The various lines it is possible to produce with a single pencil.

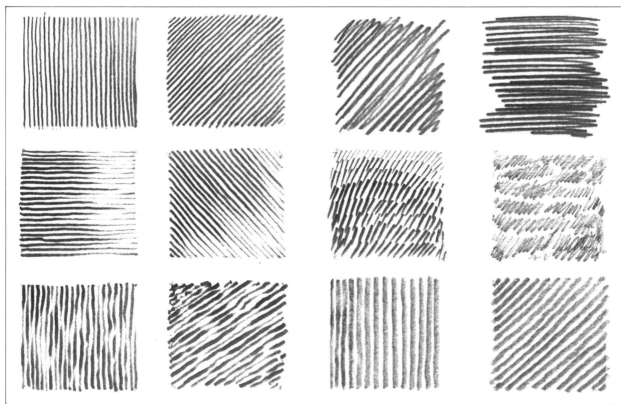

Many different kinds of line can be drawn with the same pencil. Depending on how it is held and the speed and pressure applied, it can produce a thin, sharp line like a pen, a thick, soft line and also by building up the lines, it can produce a multitude of tones, making it a very useful tool. The combined use of an eraser or tortillon and varying grades of pencil can produce a picture of remarkable depth so one should try to master the various techniques involved.

更精密的描繪
A detailed sketch.

基本的明暗表現　　　　　A sketch showing basic shading.

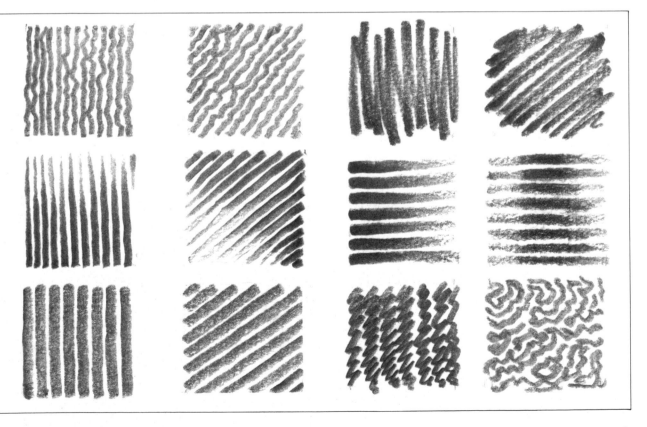

鉛筆的使用法
How to Use a Pencil

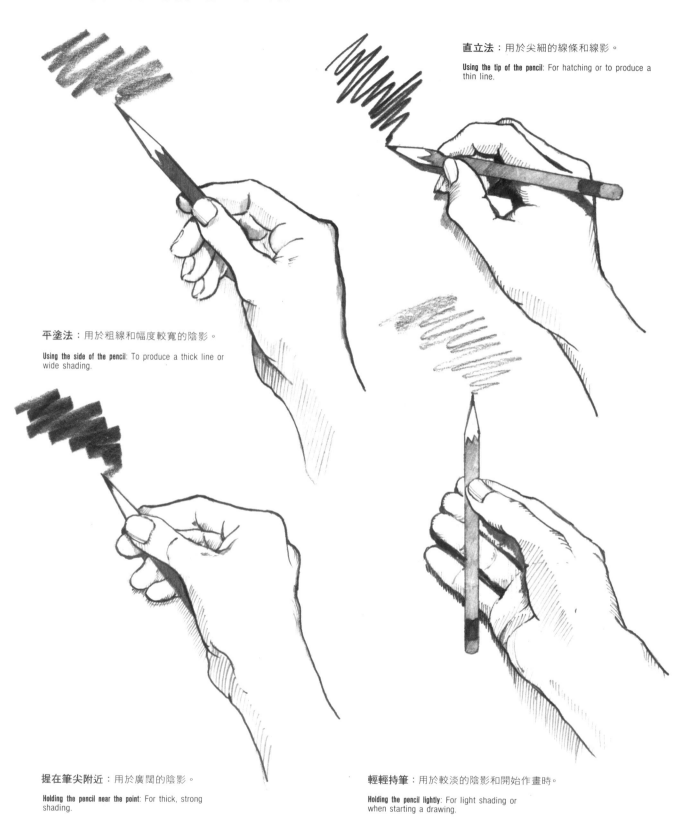

直立法：用於尖細的線條和線影。

Using the tip of the pencil: For hatching or to produce a thin line.

平塗法：用於粗線和幅度較寬的陰影。

Using the side of the pencil: To produce a thick line or wide shading.

握在筆尖附近：用於廣闊的陰影。

Holding the pencil near the point: For thick, strong shading.

輕輕持筆：用於較淡的陰影和開始作畫時。

Holding the pencil lightly: For light shading or when starting a drawing.

線條的濃淡是依筆壓的強弱，線條的粗細是依鉛筆使用法的不同來表現。一般持筆的方法，大都是接近水平，輕輕地描繪，尤其在剛開始描繪的階段，常用此方法表現大塊狀的明暗。還有使用6B軟鉛筆時，開始時不用直立法，這無法在畫紙上表現出較濃的陰影。

The depth of tone is controlled by the pressure on the pencil and the thickness of the line is controlled by the way the pencil is held. Generally the pencil is held at an angle to the paper and a gentle pressure applied. This method of holding the pencil is useful for drawing the initial outline or filling in the rough shading, but when using a soft pencil like a 6B it should be held vertical to the paper or a dark shading can not be achieved.

用平塗法畫好的部份

Drawn using the side of the pencil.

用直立法畫出線影

Hatching done with the point of the pencil.

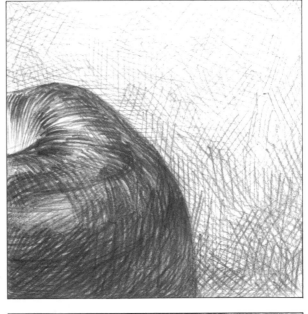

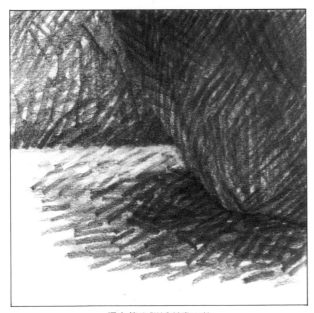

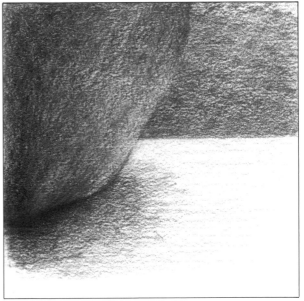

握在筆尖附近所畫出的

Drawn holding the pencil at the point.

輕輕持筆所畫出的

Drawn holding the pencil lightly.

11

筆勢和筆壓
Vigor and Pressure

無筆勢

An example of a sketch without vigor.

筆壓弱

An example of a sketch produced with little pressure.

筆勢強

An example of a sketch with vigor.

筆壓強

An example of a sketch produced with heavy pressure.

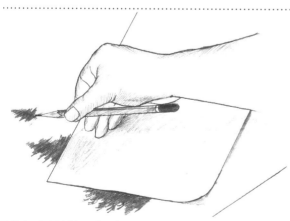

可鋪上一張薄紙在已畫好的部份，以免在畫其他部份時因手的磨擦而弄髒。

A piece of thin paper is placed over the picture to prevent the previously drawn areas from being smudged.

避免摩擦畫面，可用小指當支撐，懸空描畫。

Use the little finger as an axial one and lift up your palm. Drawing in this style the surface remains clean.

筆勢　所謂有筆勢的線是指以快速畫出的線條。如果是小心平滑地畫的話，就沒有筆勢。一般筆勢強的線條，可表現動感和速度感。

筆壓　所謂的筆壓就是鉛筆壓在紙上的壓力，可表現線條的強弱和濃淡，一般硬的物體用強筆壓來描繪，軟的物體用弱筆壓來描繪。在鉛筆素描時，請多多練習筆勢和筆壓的技法。

Vigaor: When a line is drawn rapidly, it is said to have vigor while a carefully drawn line does not. Vigor is used in a drawing to bring out a feeling of speed or motion.

Pressure: The pressure used to create a line affects its density and so by altering the pressure on the pencil as you draw, it is possible to produce graduations of light and dark. A hard object is generally drawn using heavy strokes whereas a soft object is drawn using lighter strokes. In producing a pencil drawing, it is necessary to have a good understanding of both these techniques, vigor and pressure.

使用筆勢的效果：先畫出單純的外形，再用較強的筆勢畫出動作感和速度感。

An example of a sketch making good use of vigor: Draw the basic subject, then add dynamic lines to give an impression of movement.

13

橡皮擦
Using an Eraser

畫法上的輔助畫材 在鉛筆素描中，橡皮擦和軟橡皮擦不只是拭擦用具，還可以用來表現明暗。用鉛筆難以表現的微妙明暗以及利用白紙的白色來強調光線，都可用它來表現。

An ordinary eraser and soft rubber eraser are very useful tools that can be used when producing a pencil sketch. They are not used solely for erasing lines, but also for producing very delicate tones and lifting out highlights.

用橡皮擦擦亮（上），用軟橡皮擦擦亮（下）。

A highlight lifted out with an Plastic Eraser (top). A highlight lifted out with an Rubber Eraser (bottom).

塑料橡皮擦

Plastic Eraser.

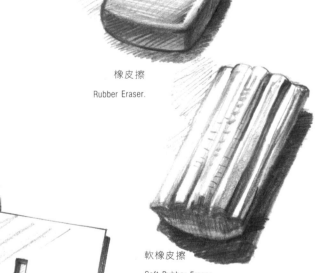

橡皮擦

Rubber Eraser.

切尖橡皮擦，以利細微的擦拭。

Erasers can be cut to a fine point for delicate erasing.

軟橡皮擦

Soft Rubber Eraser.

用紙型版擦亮。

Erasing through a paper template.

把軟橡皮擦揉成適當大小。

Tear off a suitably sized piece of soft eraser.

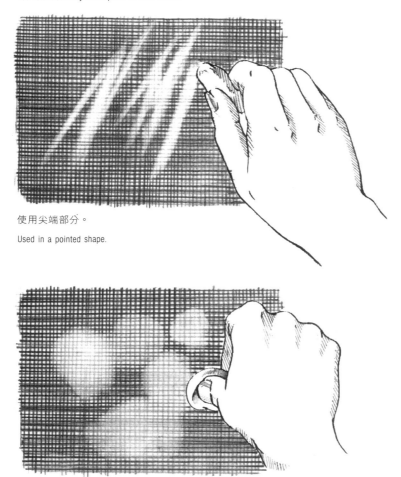

使用尖端部分。

Used in a pointed shape.

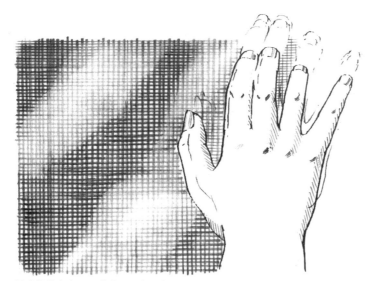

壓成圓形。

Pressed on the paper in a round shape.

揉成棒狀在畫面上滾動，可得到相同亮度的效果。

Rolled in a stick shape over the paper to produce even shading.

軟橡皮擦的使用方法。

Ways of using a soft eraser.

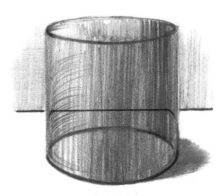

1.用鉛筆塗上陰影。

1. Shading added with a pencil.

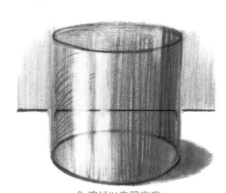

2.擦拭以表現亮度。

2. A highlight lifted out with an eraser.

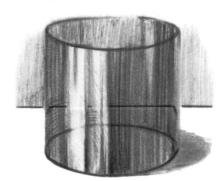

3.用鉛筆修飾留白的邊緣。

3. The edges of the highlight added with the pencil.

15

紙 筆
Using a Tortillon

紙筆在烘托鉛筆畫的明暗時，非常方便。這種技法可使鉛筆的粒子非常滑順地暈散開來。但是過份擦拭時會破壞紙質表面，再用鉛筆描繪時，就很難畫好。在素描的最後階段，可以發揮很好的效果。

只用HB畫陰影，紙筆擦拭後的效果。

Shading with an HB pencil alone and after being blurred with a tortillon.

紙筆

Tortillon.

弄髒的話，用美工刀削除。

Once the tip of the tortillon has become soiled, it can be removed with a cutter.

只用4B鉛筆的陰影，紙筆擦拭後的效果。

Shading with a 4B pencil alone and after being blurred with a tortillon.

可用面紙或布來代替紙筆做大面積的擦拭。

Tissue paper or cloth can be used in the place of a tortillon to blur a large area.

用紙筆擦拭後，再用美工刀劃出尖銳的明暗線條。

After the tone has been blurred with a tortillon, a cutter blade can be used to produce sharp highlights.

A tortillon is a tightly rolled piece of paper that can be sharpened to a point and used to blur shading. It achieves this by smearing the graphite particles on the paper but too much pressure flattens the surface of the paper making it difficult to draw over the area again. It can be used to best effect if it is left until the very end.

斜線部份用紙筆擦拭，然後再用5B鉛筆以直立法描出形狀。

The diagonal hatching was blurred with a tortillon and then the details added on top with a 5B pencil.

素描用紙
Drawing Paper

鉛筆在一般的紙上都可以作畫，除非像銅版紙一樣表面非常光滑是不適用的。紙質表面凹凸清晰的素描紙、水彩紙、木炭紙都可使鉛筆的粒子附著在凹凸的部份，容易顯出明暗是最適合素描用。但是在沒有凹凸的肯特紙上，鉛筆的粒子完全重疊，很難表現出明暗感，但是很適合非常細膩的素描。

畫板和素描紙 Carton and Drawing Paper.

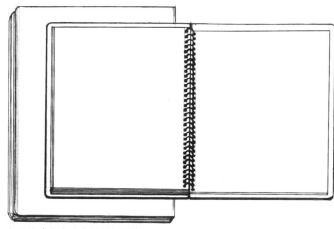

寫生簿（有各式各類的紙質）
Sketch Book. (There are many types, using various papers)

素描紙：紙的表面有凹凸。
Drawing paper: It has a rough texture.

肯特紙：紙的表面無凹凸。
Kent paper: It has no texture.

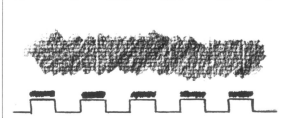

輕輕地塗上陰影。只附著於凸起的部份。

Light shading has been applied which only covers the raised part of the grain

塗上陰影。鉛筆粒子附著在紙面上。

Shading. The graphite covers the surface.

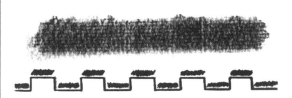

用手指揉擦。鉛筆粒子進入紙面的凹下部份。

If it is blurred with the finger, the graphite goes down into the depressions.

再塗上陰影。鉛筆粒子附著在先前的鉛筆粒子層上面。

Further shading and the graphite builds up on the previous layer.

A pencil can be used to draw on nearly any paper surface except the exceptionally shiny ones like art paper. Paper with a strong texture like drawing paper, water color paper, or charcoal paper are suitable for sketching as the graphite covers both the high and the low sections of the grain, making it easy to blend the tones. On the other hand, with smooth paper like Kent paper, it is difficult vary the shading, but with perseverance, it is possible to produce some very delicate shading so this is suitable for detailed pencil drawing.

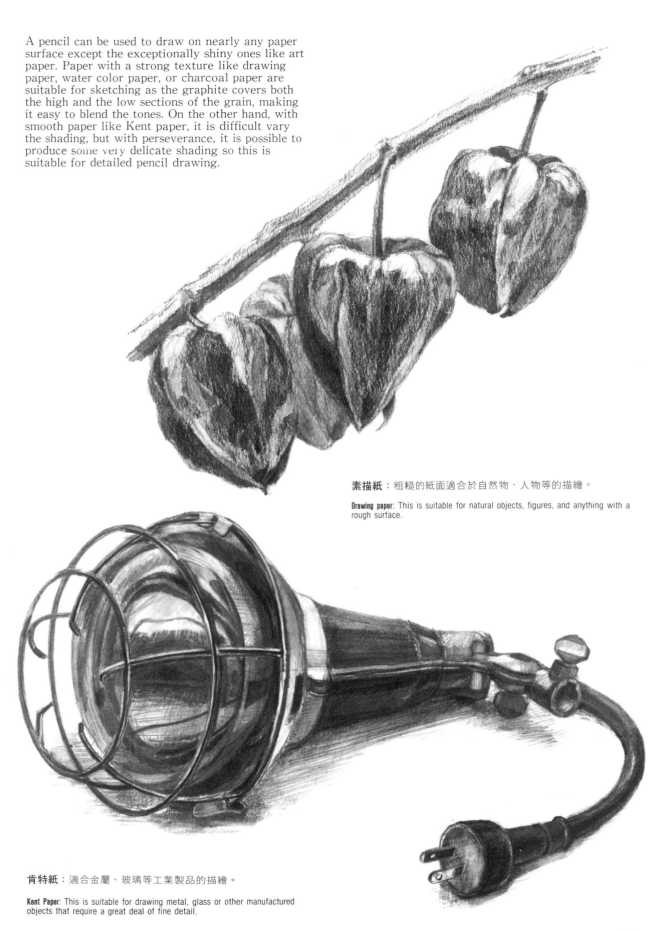

素描紙：粗糙的紙面適合於自然物、人物等的描繪。

Drawing paper: This is suitable for natural objects, figures, and anything with a rough surface.

肯特紙：適合金屬、玻璃等工業製品的描繪。

Kent Paper: This is suitable for drawing metal, glass or other manufactured objects that require a great deal of fine detail.

鉛筆素描所使用的畫材
Articles Used in Pencil Drawing

附件：鋏子是將畫紙固定在畫板上之用。在作畫時，將2～3張的畫紙墊在畫板下面，當做底墊較容易繪畫。羽毛刷用來清除橡皮擦的殘屑。固定膠可保護完成後的畫面（噴霧式）。比例尺框可把對象收入框裏，測量比例尺寸之用。

Accessories: The clip is used to fix the paper to the drawing board. When drawing, it is best to place about 2 sheets of drawing paper under one that is being used as this will act as a cushion and make it easier to draw.
The feather brush is useful to brush away the bits left by the eraser.
The fixatif enables you to protect your picture once it has been completed. (Spray type)
The ruler is useful to measure the proportions in order to scale the subject down to fit onto the paper.

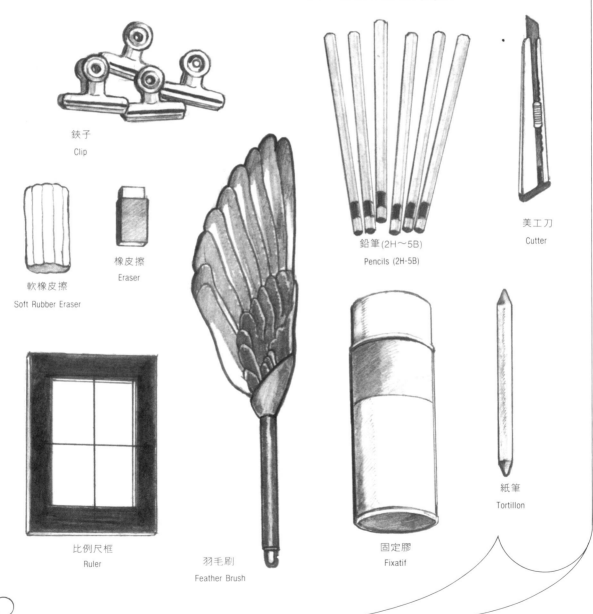

鋏子
Clip

軟橡皮擦
Soft Rubber Eraser

橡皮擦
Eraser

鉛筆(2H～5B)
Pencils (2H-5B)

美工刀
Cutter

比例尺框
Ruler

羽毛刷
Feather Brush

固定膠
Fixatif

紙筆
Tortillon

第 2 章
素描的基礎

Chapter 2
Drawing Basics

正確地描繪
In Order to Draw Accurately

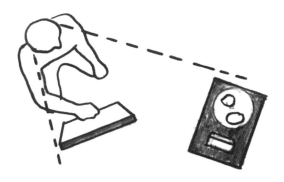

素描的姿勢：爲了能正確地描繪，畫者的身體應正對著對象，而且頭部不動，只動眼睛就可看到對象和畫紙的正確位置。坐在椅子上繪畫時，兩腿不要交叉、往後坐深一點，背部伸直，時間久的話，也不會疲倦。

物體和畫面的關係：要正確地描繪物體的形狀或位置，最基本的是要經常一面比對物體和畫面，一面進行描繪。例如，先在畫面上設定好垂直和水平的基準，然後再以此和物體比較而進行描繪，也是不錯的方法。

物體的位置：將物體和畫面擺在很輕鬆就可看見的視野內。

The Position of the Subject: The subject should be positioned so both it and the picture can be seen without any effort.

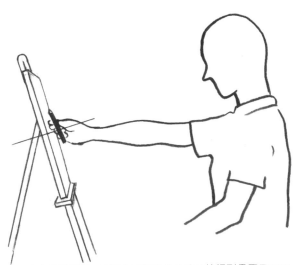

畫面和身體的距離：手腕伸直時很自然地可接觸到畫面正中央的距離。

The Distance from the Picture: The easel should be placed so that when the arm is extended, it falls in the center of the paper.

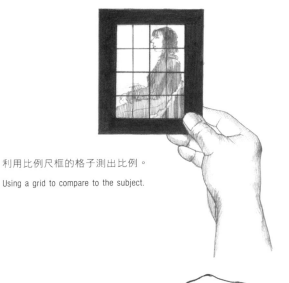

利用比例尺框的格子測出比例。

Using a grid to compare to the subject.

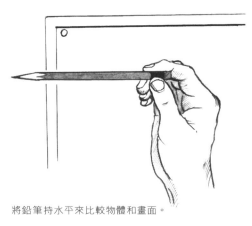

將鉛筆持水平來比較物體和畫面。

Using a pencil to see the horizontal when comparing the picture to the   subject.

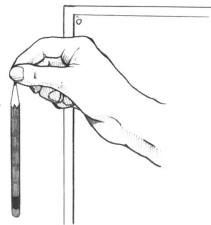

輕輕捏住筆尖做成垂直線。

Holding a pencil lightly by the tip to see the vertical.

利用硬幣和線來做成垂直線。

Suspending a coin by a thread to see the vertical.

Drawing position. In order to draw accurately, one should sit facing the subject and be able to view both the subject and the picture by only moving the eyes, not the whole head. When sitting, do not cross your legs but sit back in the chair and keep the back straight. This will allow you to draw for a long time without becoming fatigued.

The Relationship Between the Subject and Drawing. In order to draw the shape and position of the subject accurately, it is necessary to repeatedly check the drawing against the subject. One way of achieving this is to establish the vertical and horizontal planes on the picture and check these against the subject.

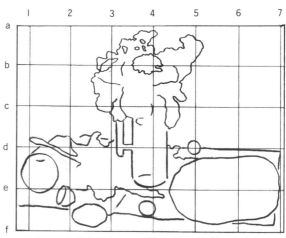

把畫面用格子等份分割，來檢查物體的位置和形狀。

A grid on the picture to check positioning.

比較明部和暗部的平衡。

Comparing the balance of the light and dark areas.

檢查背景和枱面的留白部份來和物體比對一下。

Checking the base and background areas against the subject.

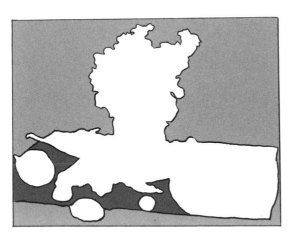

以平面式的輪廓影像來檢查畫面上的大小。

Looking at the silhouettes to check the scale of the objects on the paper.

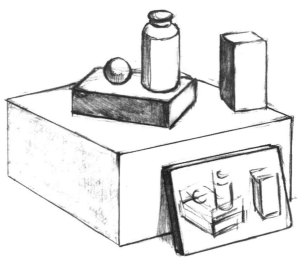

將畫面和實物比較。

Checking the subject and the picture.

23

隱藏的形狀
Hidden Shapes

請抓準繪畫者眼睛所看到枱前和最深處的距離，決定底部（斜線部份）和繩線的接地點。枱前到遠處的距離過長的話整個台座會失去水平向前傾斜。

The distance from the front of the base to the rear as seen from the artists point of view should be decided and the bases of the objects (shaded areas) drawn in. The points where the string actually touches the table (shown by the arrows) should be firmly grasped.

If the distance from the front of the picture to the rear is too long, it will be impossible to make the base look flat and it will seem to lean forwards.

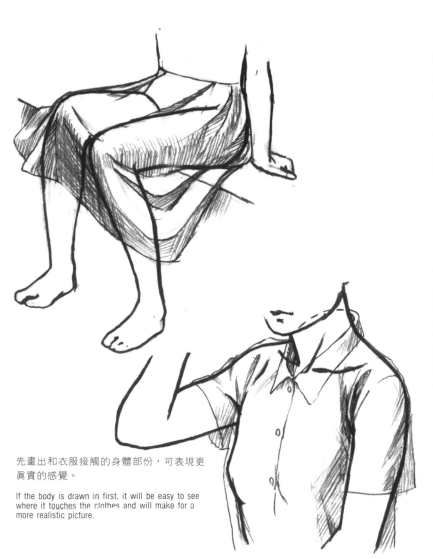

在素描時，有一個很重要的關鍵是，雖然物體藏在裏面或被包起來，眼睛看不見，但一定要表現出物和物接合部份的形狀。在描繪平台上擺著複數的靜物時，要抓好各個物體的位置關係及距離感。基本上從物體和枱面接觸的地方來決定即可。

When sketching, it is important to draw in the outlines even of objects that are covered or hidden behind another object. When drawing complicated still-life, it is important to grasp the exact positioning and relationship of the objects to each other and in order to achieve this, the areas touching the base should be drawn in first.

先畫出和衣服接觸的身體部份，可表現更真實的感覺。

If the body is drawn in first, it will be easy to see where it touches the clothes and will make for a more realistic picture.

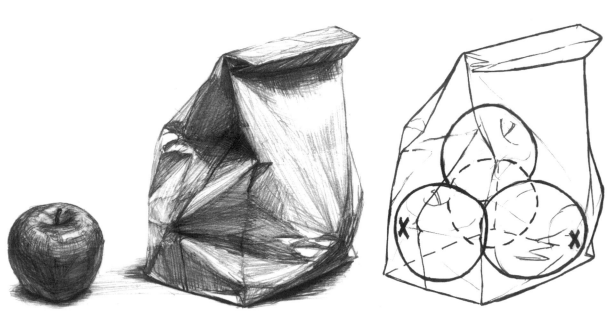

為了要表現袋中的內容物，一定要畫出蘋果和袋子接觸點（Ｘ記號）的外形。

In order to show what the bag contains, it is necessary to grasp the areas where the apples push against it (marked with an 'X').

圓和橢圓
Circles and Ovals

帶有圓形的物體，它的圓有時被畫成橢圓。基本上，橢圓的中心軸是和橢圓本身的長軸垂直的。不守這原則的話，會轉的車輪也變成不能轉。瓶身也會變得傾斜。

A circular object changes to an oval one when it is drawn, but care must be taken to draw the vertical axis at right-angles to the horizontal axis, or a bottle will become crooked and a wheel will cease to turn.

從正面正看圓柱形

A cylinder viewed from the side.

視點的高度和橢圓的變化：橢圓形長軸的長度是一定的，扁平的短軸長度會有變化。

The distortion of the oval depending on the height of the point of view: the diameter of the horizontal axis remains the same, but the vertical axis changes.

從正上面看圓柱形。

A cylinder viewed from the top.

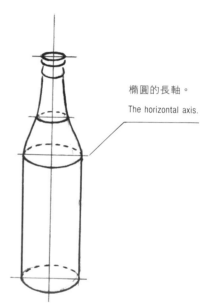

橢圓的長軸。

The horizontal axis.

橢圓的中心軸和長軸垂直。

The center axis of an oval must cross the horizontal axis at right-angles.

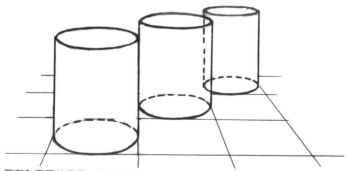

距離和橢圓的變化：距離愈遠時，長軸和短軸會變得愈短。在大圓柱的橢圓，頂部橢圓的短軸較短，底部橢圓的短軸較長，是不一樣的。

Distance and the oval: As the object moves into the distance, both the diameter and the minor axis shrink. Note that in the case of the largest cylinder, the top oval (minor axis is short) and the bottom oval (minor axis is long) are different.

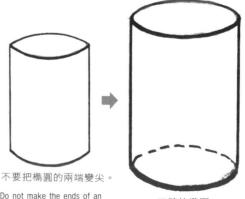

不要把橢圓的兩端變尖。

Do not make the ends of an oval too sharp.

正確的橢圓。

A correct oval.

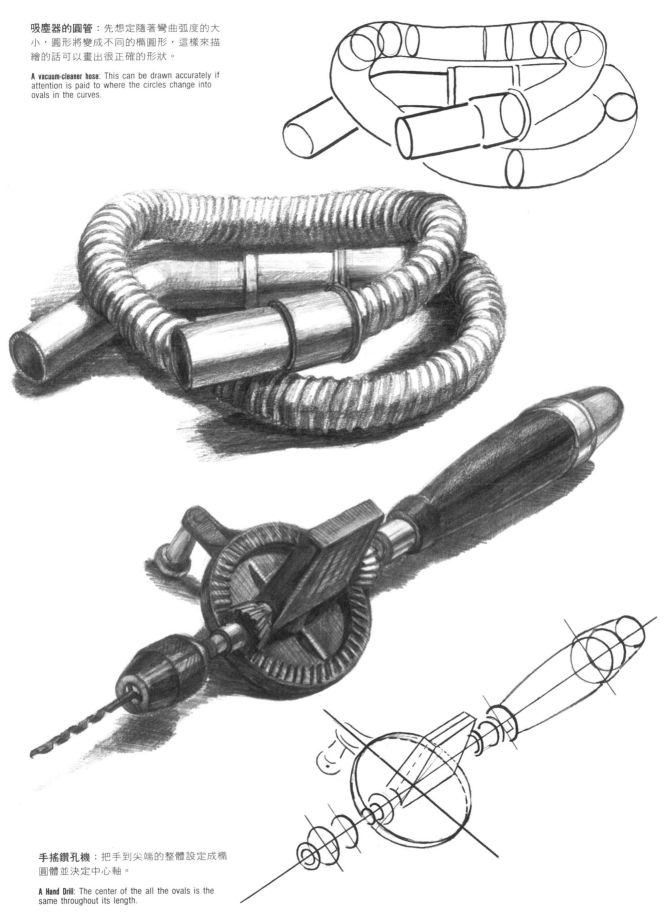

吸塵器的圓管：先想定隨著彎曲弧度的大小，圓形將變成不同的橢圓形，這樣來描繪的話可以畫出很正確的形狀。

A vacuum-cleaner hose: This can be drawn accurately if attention is paid to where the circles change into ovals in the curves.

手搖鑽孔機：把手到尖端的整體設定成橢圓體並決定中心軸。

A Hand Drill: The center of the all the ovals is the same throughout its length.

正中線
The Median Plane

所謂的正中線是指沿著人體或生物體的中心，左右分割的線。素描時以正中線爲基準，就很容易畫出人物複雜的姿勢及形態。

People and other living things can be divided down the center into two equal halves and this line is known as the Median Plane. If you use this plane as a base, it becomes much easier to sketch people in the most complicated poses.

頭部正中線的變化　　Variations in the Median Plane of the head.

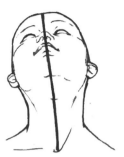

往上看

Looking up.

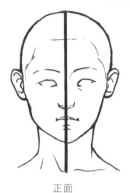

正面

Straight on.

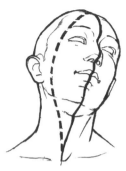

傾斜往上看（點線表示後頭部的正中線）。

Looking diagonally upwards (The dotted line indicates the median line of the rear of the head).

人體的正中線

The median plane of the human body.

正面

From the front.

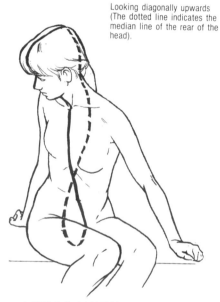

人體轉身的姿勢（點線是背部的正中線）。

With the body twisted. (The dotted line indicates the median line of the rear of the body).

魚的正中線

The Median Plane of a fish.

正中線隨著魚體而變化。

The Median Plane follows the center of the body.

魚體側面的正中線。

The Median Plane on the side of the body.

自然物的結構
The Construction of Natural Objects

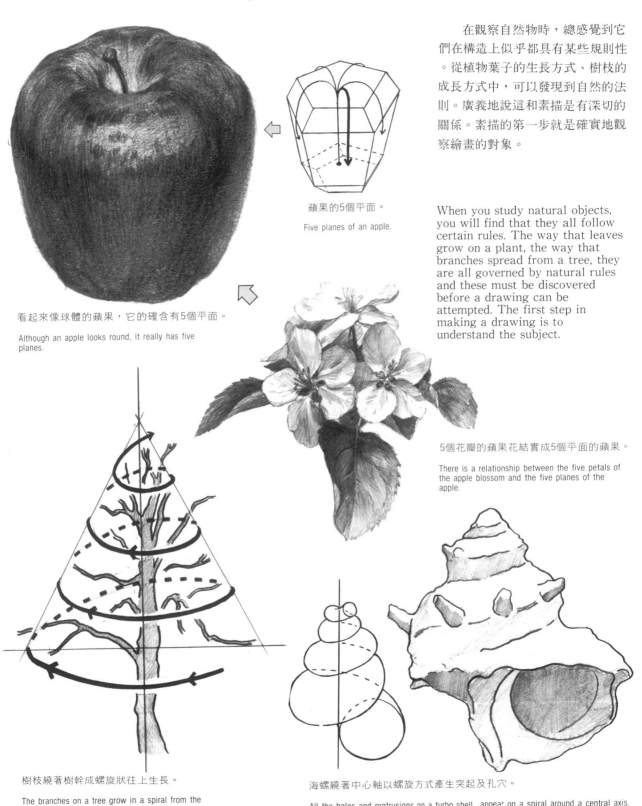

在觀察自然物時，總感覺到它們在構造上似乎都具有某些規則性。從植物葉子的生長方式、樹枝的成長方式中，可以發現到自然的法則。廣義地說這和素描是有深切的關係。素描的第一步就是確實地觀察繪畫的對象。

When you study natural objects, you will find that they all follow certain rules. The way that leaves grow on a plant, the way that branches spread from a tree, they are all governed by natural rules and these must be discovered before a drawing can be attempted. The first step in making a drawing is to understand the subject.

蘋果的5個平面。

Five planes of an apple.

看起來像球體的蘋果，它的確含有5個平面。

Although an apple looks round, it really has five planes.

5個花瓣的蘋果花結實成5個平面的蘋果。

There is a relationship between the five petals of the apple blossom and the five planes of the apple.

樹枝繞著樹幹成螺旋狀往上生長。

The branches on a tree grow in a spiral from the trunk.

海螺繞著中心軸以螺旋方式產生突起及孔穴。

All the holes and protrusions on a turbo shell appear on a spiral around a central axis.

表現形態的筆法
Touches to Illustrates Shape

雖然在物體上沒有筆法存在，但是在鉛筆素描裏，可以利用筆法表現出方向和形態。例如，物體在前光狀態，僅有一點陰影時，要將白色的物體表現出來，又不能塗得太黑，這時候使用筆法技巧是非常有效的。

Although the subject does not really have any shading, this technique is used in pencil drawing to illustrate shape and angle. The shading has to change according to the situation, if the subject is front-lit the shading will minimal and if the subject is white, it does not want heavy, black shading on it.

基本的筆法　　　Basic Shading.

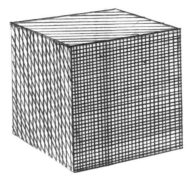

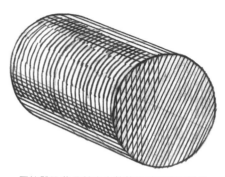

使用3種不同方向的筆法可表現出3種不同角度的平面。

Shading in three directions to illustrate the angles of the three planes.

圓柱體沿著長軸方向的筆法和沿著圓弧的筆法重疊，來加重陰影。

Shading drawn down the length of a cylinder and around the curve to accentuate its shape.

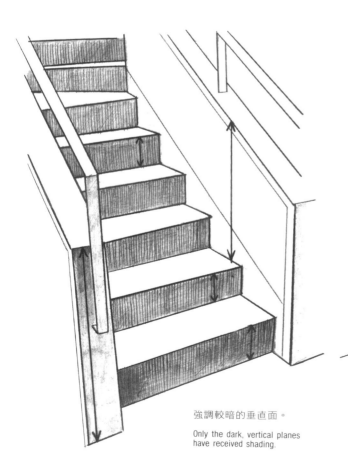

強調較暗的垂直面。

Only the dark, vertical planes have received shading.

面的方向和筆法：同一方向的面用同一方向的筆法，產生統一的感覺。如箭頭強調水平面和垂直面。

Direction of planes and Touches: Planes facing the same direction are given the same shading to produce a feeling of uniformity. The arrows show how horizontal and vertical planes have been accentuated.

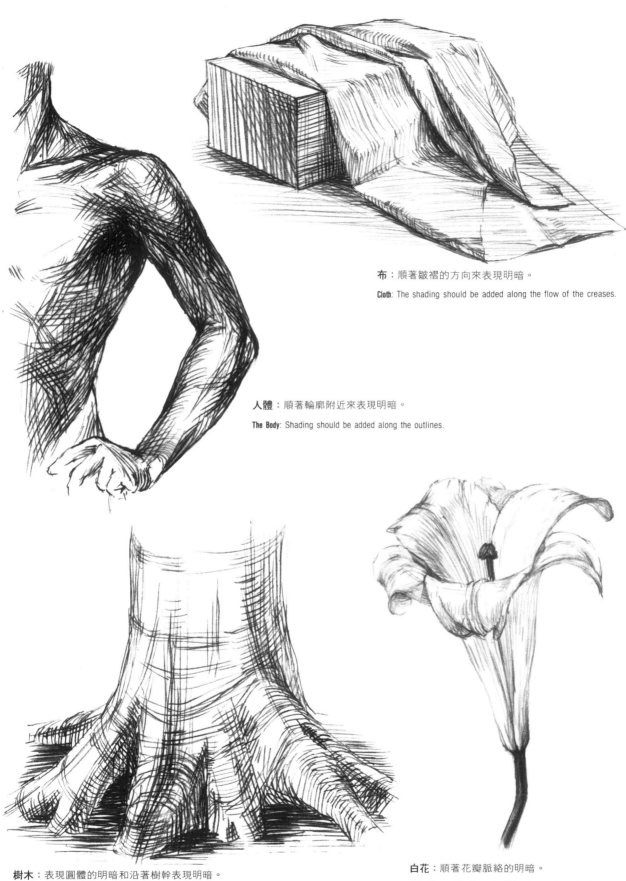

布：順著皺褶的方向來表現明暗。

Cloth: The shading should be added along the flow of the creases.

人體：順著輪廓附近來表現明暗。

The Body: Shading should be added along the outlines.

樹木：表現圓體的明暗和沿著樹幹表現明暗。

Trees: Shading is used to show the roundness and the direction of the trunk.

白花：順著花瓣脈絡的明暗。

White Flowers: Shading should be drawn down the lines of the petals.

圖樣和文字的畫法
Drawing patterns and letters

要描繪瓶子的標籤、箱子上的文字或圖樣時，一定要順著本體的形態而畫。遇到立方體或圓柱體時，最好能應用透視圖法。遇到有如布匹的質料，會產生不規則的皺褶時，一定要先把握它的基本形態，再描繪上面的模樣。

In order to draw the label on a bottle or the writing or pattern on a box, it must be remembered that the pattern has to be deformed to fit the shape of the object. In the case of a cube or cylinder, use must be made of perspective. In the case of a material like cloth where irregular folds occur, a firm grasp must be made of the basic shape before the pattern can be drawn.

平面上的文字

Letters on a Flat Surface.

折面上的文字：文字寬度的變化可用透視圖法表現出來。

Lettering on a folded surface : The width of the letters can easily be ascertained by using the rules of perspective.

捲在圓柱上的文字：在上部做同等份的圓形分割，再沿著彎曲的圓弧劃下垂直線，即可理解這種縮小的法則。

Letters wrapped around a cylindrical object: If the top of the object is split into equal sections and then lines drawn down onto the sides, it is easy to calculate how much the characters should be deformed at the edges.

打開的書本： 沿著紙面的弧度，圖樣或文字也隨著變化。

An open book: The design or lettering must curve to conform to the curve in the page.

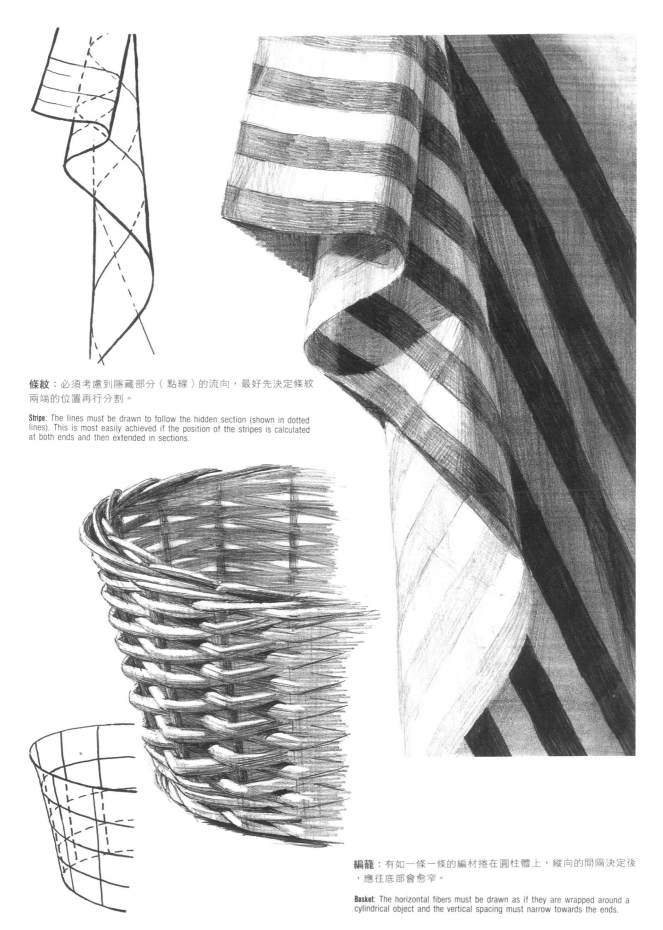

條紋：必須考慮到隱藏部分（點線）的流向，最好先決定條紋兩端的位置再行分割。

Stripe: The lines must be drawn to follow the hidden section (shown in dotted lines). This is most easily achieved if the position of the stripes is calculated at both ends and then extended in sections.

編籠：有如一條一條的編材捲在圓柱體上，縱向的間隔決定後，應往底部會愈窄。

Basket: The horizontal fibers must be drawn as if they are wrapped around a cylindrical object and the vertical spacing must narrow towards the ends.

光線的方向和陰影
The Direction of Light and Shadow

光線的方向和陰影（斜線部是影子，網點部是陰暗部）　　The Direction of Light and Shadow. (The horizontal hatching is shadow and the cross-hatching is shade)

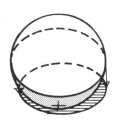 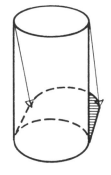 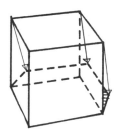

前光：這裏爲了使大家容易理解，把光線從斜上方照下來。

Front Lighting: To make this easier to see, the light has been placed high and slightly to one side.

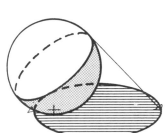 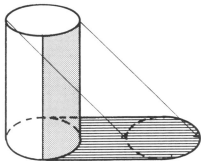

 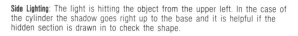

側光：光線從左上方照下的情況。圓柱的情形因爲影子和底面的圓形有接線，所以要把看不見的底面輕輕地描出來。

Side Lighting: The light is hitting the object from the upper left. In the case of the cylinder the shadow goes right up to the base and it is helpful if the hidden section is drawn in to check the shape.

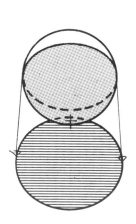 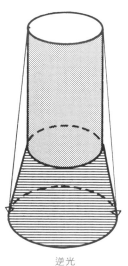 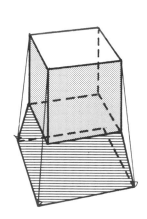

逆光

Back lighting.

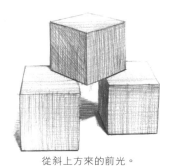

從斜上方來的前光。

Front lighting from diagonally Above.

首先，我們要理解最基本的現象，就是光的方向有3種，前光、側光（也稱順光）、逆光，而其所投射的影子的形狀也不一樣。還有影子是隨著受光面的形態而形成，在描繪影子時影子也會因被投影物的形狀而有所變化。

First it is necessary to understand that there are three basic types of lighting, front lighting, side lighting and back lighting. Also, as shadows follow the shape of the subject, it is possible to illustrate the shape of hidden objects through the use of their shadows.

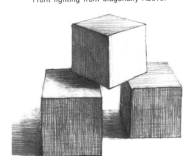

從右方來的側光。 Side lighting from the right.

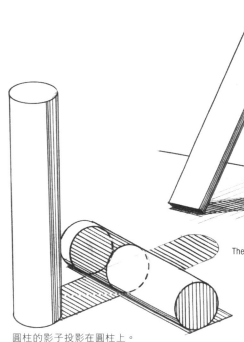

逆光　　Back lighting.

木板的影子投影在牆壁上。

The shadow of a plank leaning against the wall.

圓柱的影子投影在圓柱上。

The shadow of a vertical cylinder falling on a horizontal cylinder.

護欄的影子投影在階梯上。　　The shadow of banisters on a Stair.

素描的表現要素
Expression in Drawing

線條：平板均一無任何表現。

Lines: The lines are drawn evenly without any expression.

陰影：有明部和暗部的表現。

Shade and Shadow: Shading is added to show the areas of light and shade.

我們要強調物體的哪一部份，所用的表現方法也不一樣。在這裏舉出4種最基本的表現例子。在實際上，先畫出大概的形狀，然後再以線條來強調明暗，再加上質感。所謂素描是以好幾種表現方法併用而成的。

There are different ways of expressing the same object, depending on what you want to emphasize. In this section we will look at four different forms of expression. First the basic shape is drawn then different lines are stressed and texture added. A sketch uses several techniques simultaneously to produce the desired result.

質感：表現已塗裝過的金屬、玻璃等材質。

Material Detail: The feeling of the painted metal surface and the glass is added.

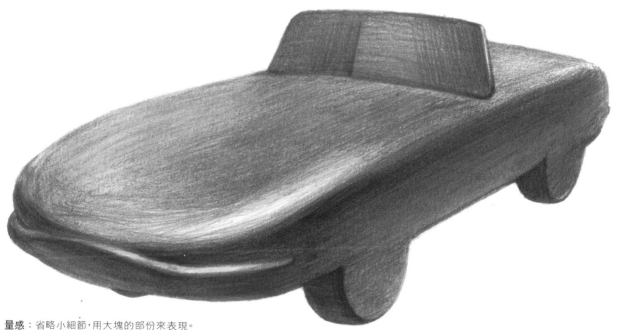

量感：省略小細節，用大塊的部份來表現。

Mass: To get a feeling of mass, the small details are excluded and it is drawn as a large block.

明暗法
Shading

明部：不觸及紙面的質地。

Area: The grain of the paper has not been flattened.

明暗的分界部：陰影不細緻還殘留著原來的紙質。

Border Between Light and Dark: The shading is not too fine and the grain of the paper still remains.

底板的反射：先畫出明暗再用紙筆擦暈，再畫上明暗。

Reflection of the Base: After the shading has been completed, it should be blurred with a tortillon then shaded again.

影子：在球的接點處塗黑變暗。

The Shadow: The area where the ball touches the base should be shaded black.

在影子的後端用軟橡皮擦壓過，紙的白色部份變得較自然。

The edge of the shadow should be softened with a soft rubber eraser to make it blend naturally with the paper.

光

Light

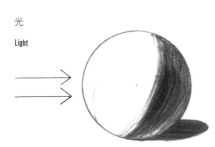

光的方向和明暗的變化：從左來的側光、逆光、前光。　Shading Differing With the Direction of the Light: Side lighting from the left, Back lighting, Front lighting.

明暗的程度可分爲明亮、中間調、黑暗3個階段。明亮程度時鉛筆粒子粗澀，視覺上物體好似凸出在眼前。黑暗程度時鉛筆粒子細膩沉著，愈黑的話會把紙紋弄平。

Shading can be broken down into three sections, light, mid-tones and dark. In the light tones the shading is very rough and visually it tends to stand to the front of a picture. The shading of dark areas is much finer and the darker it becomes, the more the grain of the paper is flattened.

明亮
Light Shading.

中間調
Mid-tone Shading.

黑暗
Dark Shading.

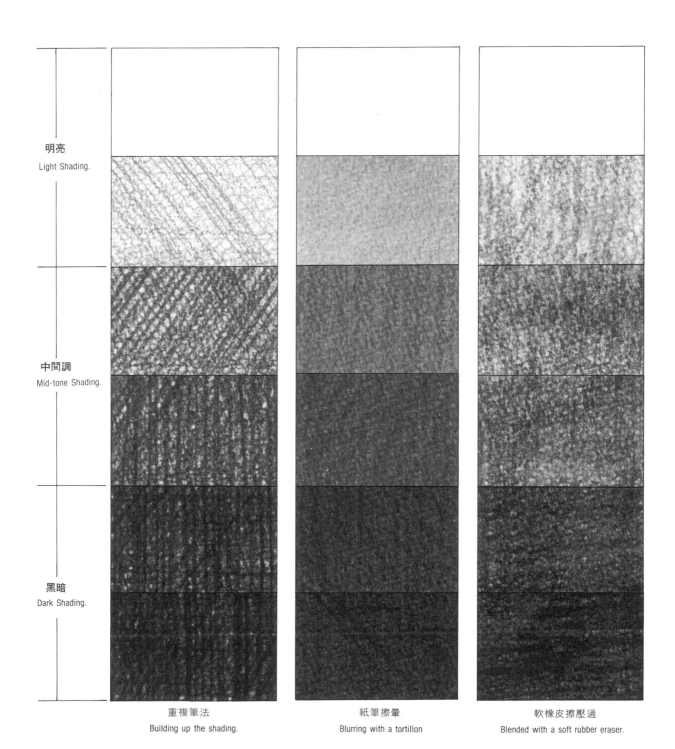

重複筆法
Building up the shading.

紙筆擦暈
Blurring with a tortillon

軟橡皮擦壓過
Blended with a soft rubber eraser.

明暗和顏色
Shading and Color

因對比而產生的變化：即使把檸檬塗上同樣的明暗，會因背景或枱面的明暗對比看起來很明亮或看起來有點灰灰的。

Utilizing Contrast: Even though it has the same shading, the lemon can look light or grey depending on its contrast with the background.

如果把顏色換成鉛筆的明暗時，濃顏色用軟鉛筆、淡顏色用硬鉛筆，這是基本的技法。還有，要使物體突顯出來時可利用淡色（明亮）和濃色（黑暗）的對比來表現。

The basic rule when depicting color in a pencil drawing is to use a soft pencil for the dark colors and a hard pencil for the lighter hues. Also, in order to pick the subject out of the background, light tones (light shading) should be contrasted with dark tones (heavy shading).

白色背景：以影子的暗色把黃色襯托出來。

White background: The dark of the shadow helps make the yellow stand out.

灰色的枱面和黑色的背景：最均衡的明暗表現。

Grey base and black background: This produces the best balance of shading.

白色的枱面和黑色的背景：襯托出檸檬的亮麗。·

White base and black background: This makes the lemon look brighter.

灰色的枱面和白色的背景：檸檬看起來好像弄髒了。

Grey base and white background: The lemon looks muddy and dirty.

檸檬：用軟鉛筆(2B)平塗法（筆心側面），筆壓減弱，使紙面粗澀表現出質感（用HB,2B）。

Lemon: Use the side of a soft pencil (2B) without much pressure to create the rough texture of the skin. (Use HB, 2B pencils)

黃色的塑膠球：用硬鉛筆利用筆勢沿著圓形球面重複地畫出陰影，可表現出光滑的質感（用2H,HB）。

Yellow Plastic Ball: Use a hard pencil to draw in the shading with vigor, following the curve of the surface to create a shiny surface. (Use 2H, HB pencils)

甜橙：用3B減弱筆壓，平塗法，利用畫紙表面的凹凸，畫出粗澀的質感（用2B,3B）。

Orange: Use the side of a 3B pencil without much pressure, utilizing the texture of drawing paper to create a rough surface. (Use 2B, 3B pencils).

深紅色的蘋果：主要用3B加強筆壓來強調圓弧的部份（用2B,3B）。

Dark Purple Grapes: Use mostly a 3B pencil. The shiny sections are formed by lifting them out with a tortil lon. (Use 3B, 4B pencils).

暗紫色的葡萄：主要用4B，光亮的部份用紙筆擦暈（用3B,4B）。

Dark Purple Grapes: Use mostly a 4B pencil. The shiny sections are formed by lifting them out with a tortillon. (Use 3B, 4B pencils).

濃淡的調子
Strong and Weak Shading

依鉛筆的軟硬不同，所表現出來的濃淡調子（素描用紙）

The Difference in Tone Between Hard and Soft Pencils. (Using Drawing Paper).

2 H	H B	2 B	6 B

即使是同樣的明度，用2H所畫出的濃淡和用6B所畫出的濃淡在質感上是不一樣的。2H會破壞紙面顯得較清脆，6B較粗有粗澀的感覺。利用這種質感的不同，像玻璃、金屬等硬質物要用硬鉛筆，布料、毛織等軟質物用軟鉛筆。

火山石（用2B,6B）：雖是粗硬的質地，但爲了表現它的黑色，而使用軟鉛筆。

Volcanic Rock: Although it is a hard rough substance, a soft pencil was used to bring out the black color. (Use 2B, 6B pencils)

Even though it may be the same brightness, shading done with a 2H pencil has a different quality to that done with a 6B. With a 2H, the grain of the paper is flattened and it has a crisp feeling whereas a 6B produces a rough textured tone. These differences in texture can be exploited, using a hard pencil for hard objects like glass or metal and a soft pencil when drawing cloth, wool and other soft items.

玻璃煙灰缸（用3H,2H,2B）：此物體大部份是中濃淡的調子，在特別濃暗的地方使用2B。

A Glass Ashtray: The mid-tone that makes up most of the object is done with a 2H pencil while a 2B was used for the darker details. (Use 3H, 2H, 2B pencils)

2H＋HB

2B

2B＋4B

2H

HB

化粧品和提袋（用2H,HB,2B,4B）：視塑料、皮革、金屬等材質的不同，使用不同的鉛筆。

A Makeup Case: Use different pencils to differentiate between the plastic, vinyl, leather and metal. (Use 2B, 2B＋4B, 2H＋HB, 2H, and HB pencils.)

質感的表現
Expressing Texture.

物體有軟、硬、有光澤、無光澤、光亮、粗澀的各種不同的質感，可依濃淡不同的對比來表現。玻璃、金屬等硬物，明暗的對比非常強烈。布料、皮膚等柔軟物，濃淡明暗的變化較緩和。

表現質感的訣竅在於：如何確實地掌握亮面和陰影變化時產生的界線、軟鉛筆和硬鉛筆所表現出的差異性；並以筆壓的強弱作不同的描繪。

金屬：明暗的變化非常極端，分別使用硬鉛筆（2H,H）和軟鉛筆(4B)，訣竅在於刺眼的光亮部份和周圍的投影。

Metal: The contrast here is quite extreme and should be reproduced using both hard (2H,H) and soft pencils (4B). The secret is to draw sharp outlines and show the reflections.

金屬的明暗　　Metal Shading.

2 H　　　　　　　　4 B　　H

混凝土：石頭或混凝土會吸收光線，不會被周圍所影響，明暗的變化比較鈍。明暗的表現，大部份用2B再用HB來處理邊緣。

Concrete: Concrete and stone absorbs the light so it does not have much influence on its surroundings and the contrast is weak. The bulk of the shading is done with a 2B pencil, an HB being used to pick out the shading at the edges.

混凝土的明暗　　　Concrete Shading.

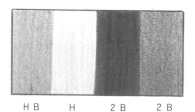

H B　　　H　　　　2 B　　　2 B

木材：要表現木質的話，用軟鉛筆（2B）畫出基本的明暗，鉛筆線之間不要太接近，空出一點空間。

Wood: To represent wood, the basic shading is done with a soft pencil (B) and the lines should not be drawn too close.

木材的明暗　　Wood Shading.

H　　　H　　　　2 B　　　2 B

There are many kinds of texture, hard, soft, shiny, rough and all these can be expressed through the use of shading. Glass, metal and other hard objects have strong contrast in the shading while soft objects like cloth or people have a soft graduation of tone.

The secret in drawing textures lies in the ability to grasp the change from highlight to shadow and to reproduce it accurately using the suitable pencil and pressure.

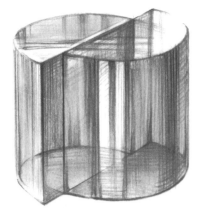

玻璃的明暗　Glass Shading.

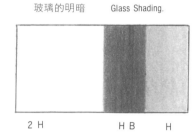

2 H　　　　H B　　H

玻璃：要表現出透明感，一定要很確實地把底邊或裏面的形狀畫出來。在光亮部份的裏面是看不見的，而在陰暗部份的底邊或裏面是可用透視看得見的。

Glass: In order to show that it is transparent, the hidden part of the base should be drawn in firmly. The further side cannot be seen in the highlights, but base and rear can be seen clearly in the shadows.

土塊：黑色而鈍的泥土會吸光，明暗的變化較小。使用軟鉛筆，在黑色部份的明暗，可做不同變化的處理。

Earth: Dull, black earth absorbs all the light so there is very little change in the shading. Look for a black area in the subject that can be used to give the shading some variety.

泥土的明暗　Earth Shading.

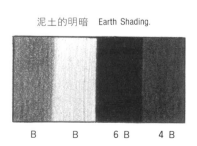

B　　　B　　　6 B　　4 B

紙捲：要表現白色和軟硬度，減低筆壓，使用緩和的明暗變化。亮部用硬鉛筆(H)，暗部用軟鉛筆(B,2.B)。

Paper: In order to represent the whiteness and hardness of the paper shading should be done without much pressure, allowing the pencil to slide lightly over the paper. A hard pencil (H) should be used for the light areas and a B or HB for the shadows.

紙的明暗　Paper Shading.

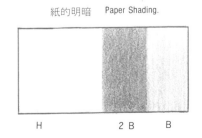

H　　　　2 B　　　B

衣服的質感
The Texture of Clothes

最重要的是稍微誇張地把皺褶或織紋的地方，強調其明暗的微妙變化。這時用軟鉛筆用平塗法加筆壓，重複畫好幾次，最後用軟橡皮擦處理光亮的部份。

The important point when drawing clothes is to exaggerate the weave or creases of the materials used. Use the side of the lead of a soft pencil, not to applying much pressure but building up the texture gradually. Highlights can be added later through use of a soft rubber eraser.

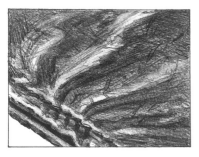

皮革：最亮部份的界線上稍微弄暈。皺褶的明暗對比非常少。

Leather: Blur the edges of the highlights, there is not very much difference of contrast in the undulations caused by creases.

斜紋棉布：強調織紋的紋樣，一部份用明暗的手法表現。

Denim: Exaggerate the pattern of the weave, supply variety by adding light and dark tones in the clothes.

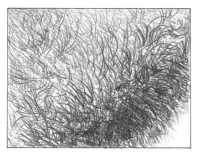

毛皮：以重複多次的方式，畫出柔軟的細毛，並賦與明暗的變化。

Fur: Go over the same area repeatedly, building up the image of soft hairs, differentiating between light and shade.

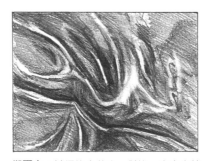

塑膠布：皺褶比皮革多，對比、亮度也較強。

Plastic cloth: It has more creases than leather and the contrast and highlights are both strong.

綿布：白布的話，用水平法輕輕地畫出皺褶的明暗，用背景來強調明暗度的差別。

Cotton: To draw the creases in white material, use the side of the pencil and press very lightly. Exaggerate the difference in brightness between the object and the background.

較薄的質地：先畫出透視下可以看見的皺褶、圖樣，再重疊畫上去。

Thin material: Draw the creases and patterns on the bottom layer first, then draw the semi-transparent top layer.

絲絨：先將整體畫上暗色調子，再疊畫上更黑的陰影，然後在皺褶的亮光處；軟橡皮擦處理。

Velvet: Shade in a dark tone overall then add darker shadows on top. The highlights in the folds can be added later with a soft rubber eraser.

編織：在某些部份強調編織的紋樣，其餘的部份用中間調來處理重複的紋樣。

Knitware: Exaggerate areas of the stitches and fill the remainder with mid-tones.

編織
Knitware

皮革
Leather

毛皮
Fur

47

蔬菜的質感
The Texture of Vegetables

基本上先確實地把握住全體的形態，再畫出質感。因為表皮的凹凸和質地的不同，而使用明暗的技法也不一樣。以均一質感似的全面性描繪是不行的。

要將物體的特徵，表現得引人注目，也就要看你質感表現得如何了？為了能成功地表現物體的特徵，不同的質感應使用不同的技法，更能得到整體的諧調，也就是一幅好的素描。

青椒：顏色濃有光澤，凹凸的地方明暗的表現要能把握住陰影和反射的法則。

Pepper: A pepper has a rich color and lustre. The tones in the depressions should take into account the shadows and reflections. (use 2B, 4B pencils)

More attention should be paid to the shape of the object as a whole than to the texture of the skin. Although the roughness of the skin texture will alter the overall tone of the picture, it should not be added in the same detail over the whole object. The characteristics features of the object should be exaggerated, even at the cost of texture detail, and by using texture selectively, it is possible to accentuate the characteristics of the object and produce a a more satisfying sketch.

面的角度和陰影的關係　The connection between angles and shadow.

陰　Shadow.

反　Reflection shadow.

影　Shade.

陰　Shadow.

青花菜：順著葉子的起伏不平，以明暗濃淡的不同來表現，較亮的地方一粒一粒清楚地描繪。

Broccoli: Grasp the light and dark tones in the undulations and make sure that the relatively light areas are drawn clearly.

原寸大的局部圖
Detail in Actual Size.

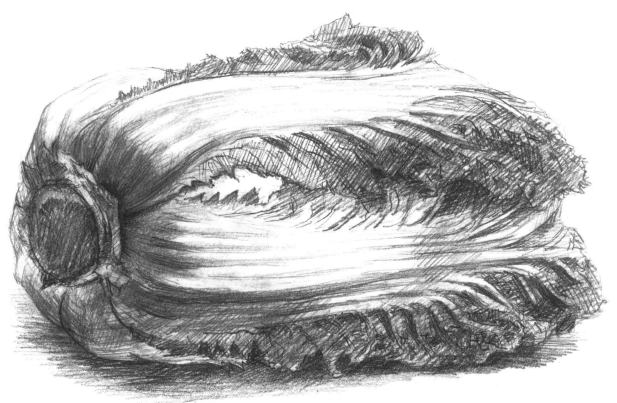

白菜：整片延伸的菜葉，它的白色部份用硬鉛筆沿著形態上的凹凸葉脈畫出明暗，其他葉子的部份用軟鉛筆先作成較粗放的明暗底層，再加上細部的明暗表現（用H,2B）。

Chinese Cabbage: The white of the leaves spreading from the stems is drawn with a hard pencil, following the shape of the leaf and stressing the ribs of he veins. The soft part of the leaf is done by filling in the detail over rough shading. (use H, 2B pencils)

部份原寸大

Detail in Actual Size.

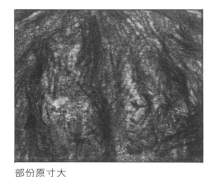

部份原寸大

Detail in Actual Size.

南瓜：整體用球體的法則畫出明暗，然後在表皮凹凸不平的地方以陰影的畫法表現（用2B,4B）。

Pumpkin: The basic toning should be that for a round object. Exaggerate the shadows formed by the skin texture in dark area. (use 2B, 4B pencil)

理解主體　Understanding the Subject

　　素描的原則是確實理解被畫的物體後，再著手作畫。例如：只從作畫的方向來看物體是不行的，儘可能改變你的視點，從正面、橫面、上方等來觀察，把握住物體的整體像。這樣的話，你就能夠理解「這個角度是這種形狀」，這將會提升你素描的能力。

One of the basic rules in sketching is, "Know your subject." For instance, when you are about to draw something, do not be content with just one view of it, you should try and get as many views as possible, from the front, the side even the top. When you know your subject as well as you are able you should be able to have a better understanding of how it will look from a certain angle.

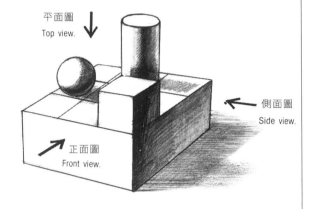

平台上的幾何形體，為了容易理解，將正方體分割為9等份。

A geometric object on a base. In order to make it easier to grasp, the base has been split into nine equal sections.

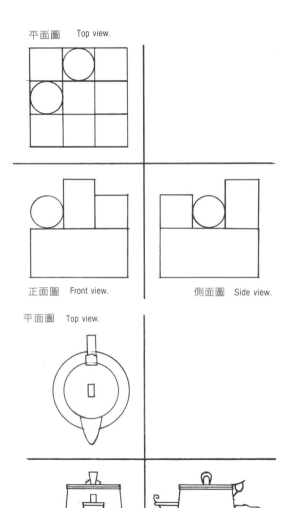

以圖形的方式來理解不銹鋼水壺的形態。

A projection of a stainless water jug.

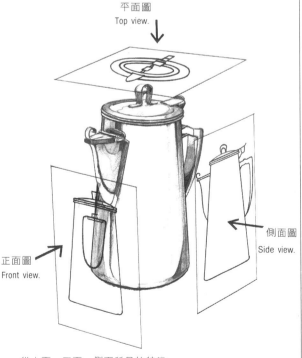

從上面、正面、側面所見的特徵。

The top, front and side views all have their own characteristics.

第 3 章
靜物素描

Chapter 3
Drawing Still-Life

花
Flowers

山茶花：因爲是白花，明暗的表現要節制。順著花瓣的弧度，畫出花朵的模樣。
（用6B，HB）

Camellias: This is a white flower so do not add too much shading. The pattern should also be drawn following the curve of the petals. (Use 6B HB pencils)

唐菖蒲：要意識到光線的方向，明亮和陰暗的區分，表現出重瓣花朵的立體感（用HB）

Gladioli: By paying attention to the direction of the light and adding shading to the light and dark areas, it is possible to achieve a feeling of depth. (Use HB pencil)

葵花：順著花瓣的弧度，從花蕊往外重覆地畫出明暗。花蕊的明亮部分用軟橡皮擦處理（用6B,3B）。

Hollyhocks: The shading on the petals is built up from the center of the flower following the curve. The highlights in the center of the flower can be lifted out carefully using a soft rubber eraser. (Use 6B, 3B pencils)

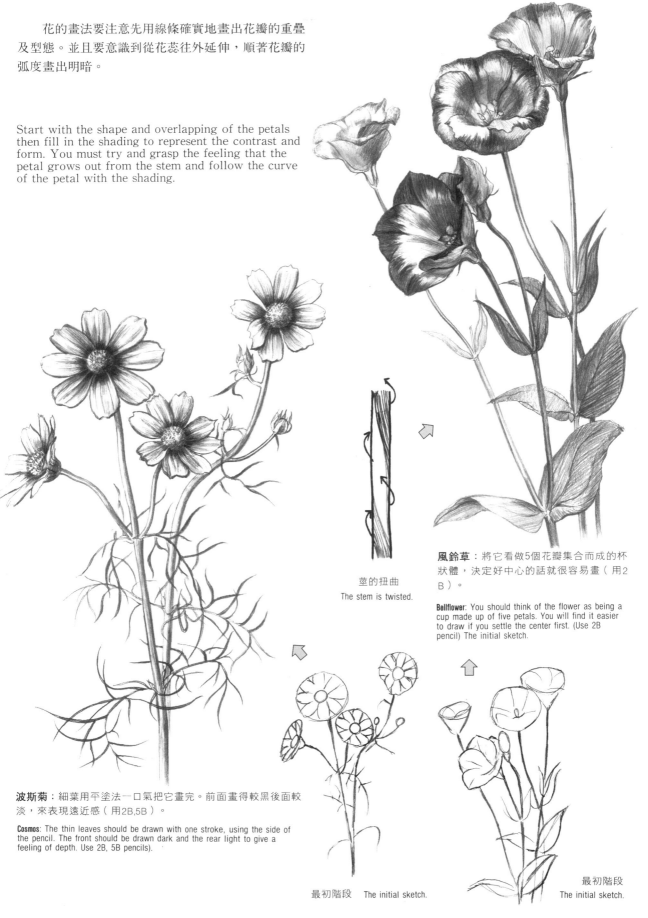

花的畫法要注意先用線條確實地畫出花瓣的重疊及型態。並且要意識到從花蕊往外延伸，順著花瓣的弧度畫出明暗。

Start with the shape and overlapping of the petals then fill in the shading to represent the contrast and form. You must try and grasp the feeling that the petal grows out from the stem and follow the curve of the petal with the shading.

莖的扭曲
The stem is twisted.

風鈴草：將它看做5個花瓣集合而成的杯狀體，決定好中心的話就很容易畫（用2B）。

Bellflower: You should think of the flower as being a cup made up of five petals. You will find it easier to draw if you settle the center first. (Use 2B pencil) The initial sketch.

波斯菊：細葉用平塗法一口氣把它畫完。前面畫得較黑後面較淡，來表現遠近感（用2B,5B）。

Cosmos: The thin leaves should be drawn with one stroke, using the side of the pencil. The front should be drawn dark and the rear light to give a feeling of depth. Use 2B, 5B pencils).

最初階段　The initial sketch.

最初階段
The initial sketch.

深色花的明暗表現

The Shading of Dark Flowers

顏色較深的花用軟鉛筆（5B, 6B）直立法，塗上黑色的調子。明亮處的對比調用軟橡皮擦壓過，處理成白色後再用鉛筆修飾。其他還可用紙筆從黑色漸漸地轉成白色。

When drawing dark flowers, use a soft pencil (5B, 6B) and hold it vertical to the paper to produce almost black shading. The lighter areas can be lifted out with a soft rubber eraser or erased entirely and then retouched with a pencil. Also a tortillon can be used to produce a smooth graduation of shading from black to white.

最初階段

The initial sketch.

爵床科觀葉植物：葉面的凹凸部分是黑色的調子，其中受光部分較亮，背光部分較暗。

Aphelandra: The texture of the leaves is shown using two tones, the black shadow and the light highlights.

向日葵：黃色的花瓣部分以簡潔，較淡的筆法畫出，花蕊要以更黑的對比表現出花的厚度。（用2B，6B）

Sunflower: The light, yellow petals are drawn with simple, light shading while by contrast, the center of the flower is drawn very dark to give the flower a feeling of bulk. (Use 2B 6B pencils)

斜方向的形狀。

A diagonal view.

正面的形狀。

A frontal view.

最初階段

The initial sketch.

石斛蘭：在一條花莖上，愈往尖端各花的距離愈窄，也愈明亮（用4B,6B）。

Dendrobium: The flowers grow in a row down the stem. As you move up the stem, the interval between the flowers decreases and shading should become lighter. (Use 4B 6B pencils)

聚合的花
Flowers in a Group

山丹花：很多明亮的小花聚在一起，成爲一個大塊，在明亮的調子中，以明暗的對比來表現（用HB,2B）。

Santanka: A group of small bright flowers can be drawn in a large block with light shading to pick out the individual petals. (Use HB 2B pencils)

最初階段

The initial sketch.

下一頁的一部分

A detail from the following page.

大丁草（菊科）：一朵白花的情況，畫出花瓣的輪廓線，聚合起來的白花，以背景的葉片明暗對比來表現。

Gerbera: When drawing a single white flower like this, the outline of the petals should be drawn in, but when drawing them in a bunch they should be represented by the contrast with the dark leaves behind them. (Use 2B 4B pencils)

灌木上的花
Flowers on a Shrub

把它看成一個大物體，畫出整體時，先把骨幹的樹枝畫出，再決定花和葉子的位置。如果有些花或葉子會損害到全體的均衡感時，把它處理成和不顯目的葉子同調，或將它省略，這樣就可以使主題的花朵更生動。

When drawing a large subject like a shrub, you should start by drawing the stem and branches which will form a framework for you to add the leaves and flowers later. The flowers and leaves that will detract from the general balance should be shaded to the same tone as the background leaves or omitted altogether and this will have the effect of making the main flowers come alive.

最初階段

The initial sketch.

用明暗的差別來表現重覆的葉子。
Use the contrast of dark and light shading to illustrative the overlapping of leaves.

描繪出花瓣彎曲的弧面（箭頭方向）。
Draw petals with slight curves (vefer to arrow marks).

芙蓉：（用2B，4B）裏面的葉子用明暗對比來表現。畫花瓣時，注意明快地畫出從花蕊往外延伸的線條。

Cotton Rose: (Use 2B 4B pencils) Use the contrast of dark and light shading to illustrate the depth of the leaves. Use light shading to illustrate the way the petals spread outwards from the stem.

最初階段
The initial sketch.

木槿：（用B,4B）枝或葉很密集的情況，
先把握住整體的明暗調子。

Althaea: (Use B, 4B Pencils) Where the branches are
very dense, use rough shading to grasp the total
shape.

把葉子看成菱形來畫。

It is useful to draw the leaves as a diamond
shape.

花的組合
Collections of Flowers

百合・玫瑰：把百合當主角，玫瑰佔第2位。將百合的方向調整，使視線順著左下方移動，使全部往上方移動的畫面，有些變化（用HB,4B）。

Lilies, Roses etc.: In this picture, the lily is the main subject and so the roses have been positioned to make them secondary to it. Instead of letting the eye drift upwards, the lily has been positioned so the direction of the flower draws the viewers attention to the bottom left. (Use HB 4B pencils)

這裏將數種花作成自由的組合，來磨練你的素描能力。把主要的花置於畫面中央，使背後感覺較清爽。還有在配置其他的花時，花朵的方向，高度最好不要太整齊，才能使畫面富於變化。

Here we have gathered several different flowers together to produce a sketch. The basic trick behind the composition is to put the main flowers in the center and to keep the background simple in order to make them stand out. When other flowers are also depicted, you should vary their height and direction to avoid the picture becoming monotonous.

紫羅蘭・匙葉草：將紫羅蘭當主角置於畫面的中央。在淡淡的白花群中，強調莖和葉的明暗，有力地描繪出往上的生長氣勢（用6B,4B,HB ）。

Stock, Statice etc.: The stock is the main subject so it has been placed in the center of the picture. In contrast to the white flowers, the stem and leaves have been given dark shading to strengthen the impression of it growing strongly upwards. (Use 6B 4B HB pencils)

描繪葉子的基本技法：當對稱的葉子扭曲，可以看到葉子的背面時，和上圖一樣，畫出中心線即可。還有，大部分的葉子表面會比背面顏色較濃，請用明暗區別出來。

The basic Technique for Drawing Leaves: When a symmetrical leaf has twisted to show the underside, it is useful to draw in the center line, as shown in this sketch. Also, in most cases, the top of a leaf is darker than the bottom and this difference should be represented in the shading.

魚貝類
Fish and Shellfish

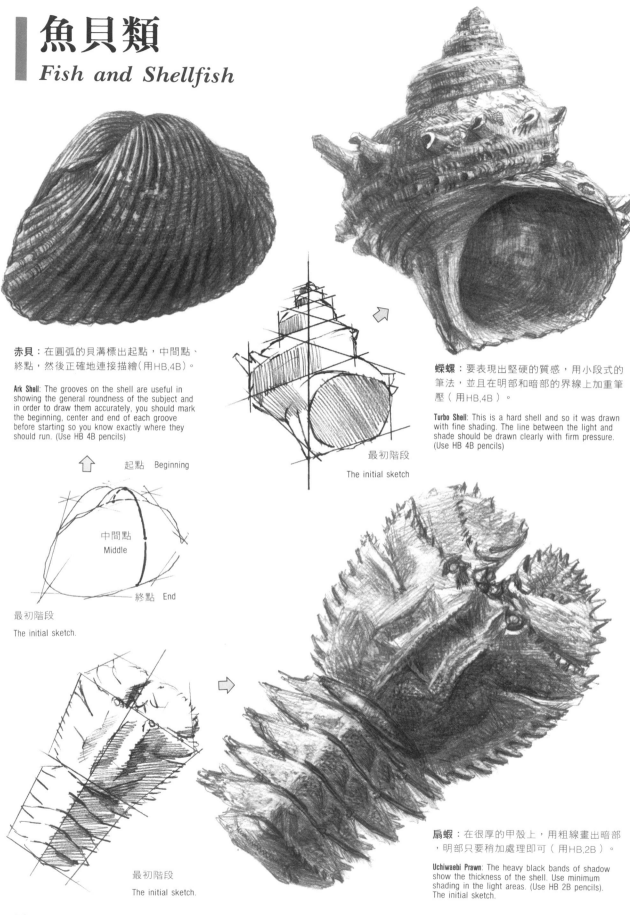

赤貝：在圓弧的貝溝標出起點、中間點、終點，然後正確地連接描繪（用HB,4B）。

Ark Shell: The grooves on the shell are useful in showing the general roundness of the subject and in order to draw them accurately, you should mark the beginning, center and end of each groove before starting so you know exactly where they should run. (Use HB 4B pencils)

起點　Beginning

中間點
Middle

終點　End

最初階段

The initial sketch.

最初階段

The initial sketch

蠑螺：要表現出堅硬的質感，用小段式的筆法，並且在明部和暗部的界線上加重筆壓（用HB,4B）。

Turbo Shell: This is a hard shell and so it was drawn with fine shading. The line between the light and shade should be drawn clearly with firm pressure. (Use HB 4B pencils)

最初階段

The initial sketch.

扇蝦：在很厚的甲殼上，用粗線畫出暗部，明部只要稍加處理即可（用HB,2B）。

Uchiwaebi Prawn: The heavy black bands of shadow show the thickness of the shell. Use minimum shading in the light areas. (Use HB 2B pencils). The initial sketch.

魚類、貝類等自然物中，即使是同一種的生物，往往在個體上是有差別的，不論在顏色或形態上都不一樣。但是在素描時，比個體上的差別更重要的是要以中心軸、構造為基礎畫出魚貝類的特徵，而重點式的表現出其形態和質感。

Even though they may be of the same species, natural subjects like fish or shellfish are each differs slightly from the others in shape or color. However, in a sketch, we are not interested in the individuality of the subject but in its texture and the construction around the median plane.

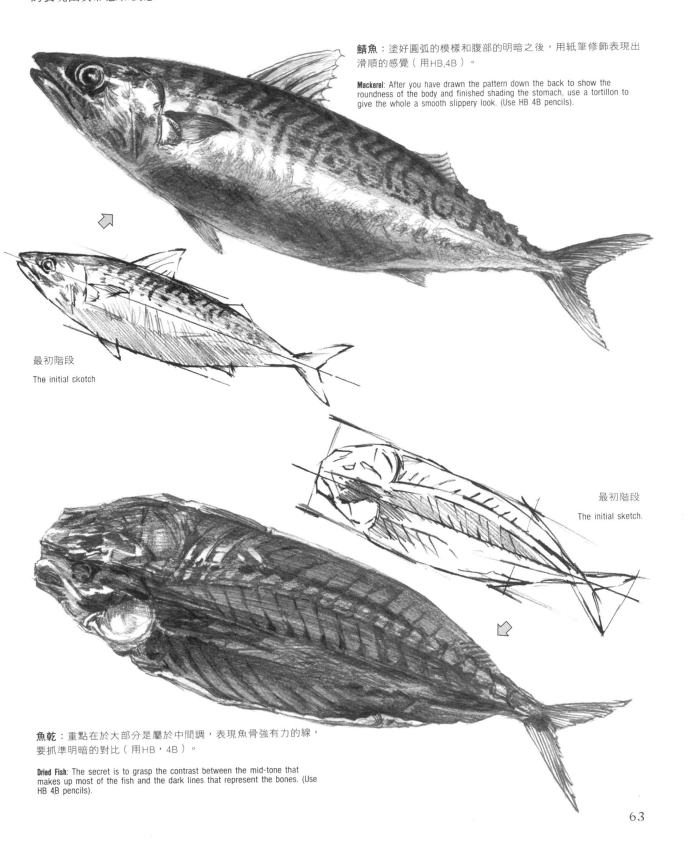

鯖魚：塗好圓弧的模樣和腹部的明暗之後，用紙筆修飾表現出滑順的感覺（用HB,4B）。

Mackerel: After you have drawn the pattern down the back to show the roundness of the body and finished shading the stomach, use a tortillon to give the whole a smooth slippery look. (Use HB 4B pencils).

最初階段

The initial ckotch

最初階段

The initial sketch.

魚乾：重點在於大部分是屬於中間調，表現魚骨強有力的線，要抓準明暗的對比（用HB，4B）。

Dried Fish: The secret is to grasp the contrast between the mid-tone that makes up most of the fish and the dark lines that represent the bones. (Use HB 4B pencils).

器 物
Containers

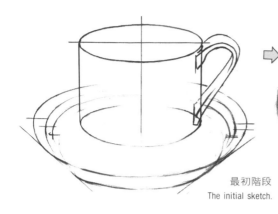

最初階段
The initial sketch.

咖啡杯：正確抓住底盤的圖樣，恰好是一個橢圓。要表現立體感，請注意右側陰暗的部分要較濃（用HB,2B,4B）。

Coffee Cup: The design on the saucer must follow the shape of the oval accurately, but in order to give a feeling of depth, the shadow should be drawn darker on the left. (Use HB 2B 4B pencils).

最初階段
The initial sketch.

陶製花瓶：圓形的圖樣在圓柱的曲面上會變形成橢圓。特別是細長的頸部上及兩側的地方會有較大的變形（用HB，3B，4B）。

A China Vase: The round design must follow the curve of the vase and become oval. The distortion is particularly noticeable in the thin neck and towards the sides. (Use HB 3B 4B pencils)

要正確地描繪基本形態是圓柱體或圓椎體的器物時，要先畫出上部和底部所形成的橢圓形及中心軸。並且確認把手的中心線會與中心軸垂直相交，這樣就可畫出正確的形態。

When drawing an object that is either conical or cylindrical in shape, it is best to draw the center axis that runs from the top to the bottom first. If there is a handle affixed to the object, a line running through its center should cross the center axis at right angles and there will be no distortion.

中心軸　central axis

最初階段　The initial sketch.

咖啡滴壺：注意把手的中心線要通過橢圓的中心軸。用直線的調子來表現玻璃的堅硬質感（用HB，2B，4B）。

Coffee Drip: Be careful to make sure that the line through the handle crosses the central axis of the jug. The hardness of the glass can be represented by using straight lines when shading. (Use HB 2B 4B pencils)

最初階段　The initial sketch.

水晶玻璃：表面上具有規則性的花樣，要細心地將每1個面的光亮、陰暗、反射一一畫出來，就能表現出質感（用HB，2B，4B）。

Cut Glass: The regular pattern of the cut should be drawn faithfully, showing the highlights, shadows and reflections of each segment. (Use HB 2B 4B pencils)

小物件
Small Articles

最初階段

The initial sketch.

鑰匙：明亮面用較清爽的調子和陰暗面作強烈的對比，這是表現金屬質感的訣竅（用HB，4B）。

Key Ring: The trick in drawing small metal objects is to have light shading on the bright areas that are contrasted with crisp, heavy shading in the shadows. (Use HB 4B pencils)

最初階段

The initial sketch.

手錶：畫小物件時，最好能畫1.5倍的大小，這樣才能確實表現出質感（用HB，4B）。

Wristwatch: When drawing small items like this, it is best to make them about 1.5 times as big as the actual object or it is difficult to express them well. (Use HB 4B pencils)

最初階段　　The initial sketch.

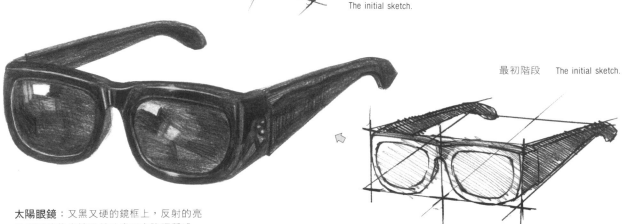

太陽眼鏡：又黑又硬的鏡框上，反射的亮光要用軟橡皮擦尖銳地處理來強調質感，並且強調鏡片上反射的光（用2B,6B）。

Sunglasses: The highlights on the hard black frame should be lifted out using a soft rubber eraser. The reflections in the lenses should serve to stress the highlights. (Use 2B 6B pencils)

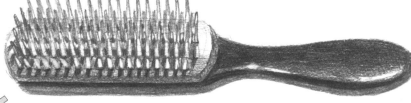

梳子：觀察一排一排不同高度的突起，強調突起的影子，並注意間隔的表現（用HB,2B）。

Hairbrush: Notice the difference in height of each row of bristles and accentuate the shadows of each bristle to stress the spacing between them. (Use HB 2B pencils)

最初階段　　The initial sketch.

家俱
Furniture

最初階段

The initial sketch.

民俗椅子：要畫出白楊木的材質感要用直立法，並把筆壓減弱。強調編繩的紋路，可表現出立體感（用HB,2B）。

Country Chair: The feeling of the poplar wood is brought out by using the pencil vertically to the paper and pressing lightly when filling in the shading. The weaving of the seat is one of the main features of the picture and the shading should be quite dark to give a feeling of depth. (Use HB 2B pencils).

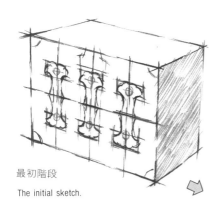

最初階段

The initial sketch.

木箱：一塊一塊的木板先用立方體的概念，賦予整體的明暗調子。表面上的木紋用硬鉛筆薄薄地描繪。黑色的鐵片用軟鉛筆，以直立法塗上平板的調子，用軟橡皮擦處理光亮部分，造成對比的效果（用2H，2B，4B）。

Chest: The wooden section is shaded as for a cube and the woodgrain is drawn in lightly with a hard pencil. The black iron is done with a soft pencil held vertically to the paper and given flat shading. Highlights can be lifted out with a soft rubber eraser to produce some contrast. (Use 2H 2B 4B pencils)

金屬材質
Metal

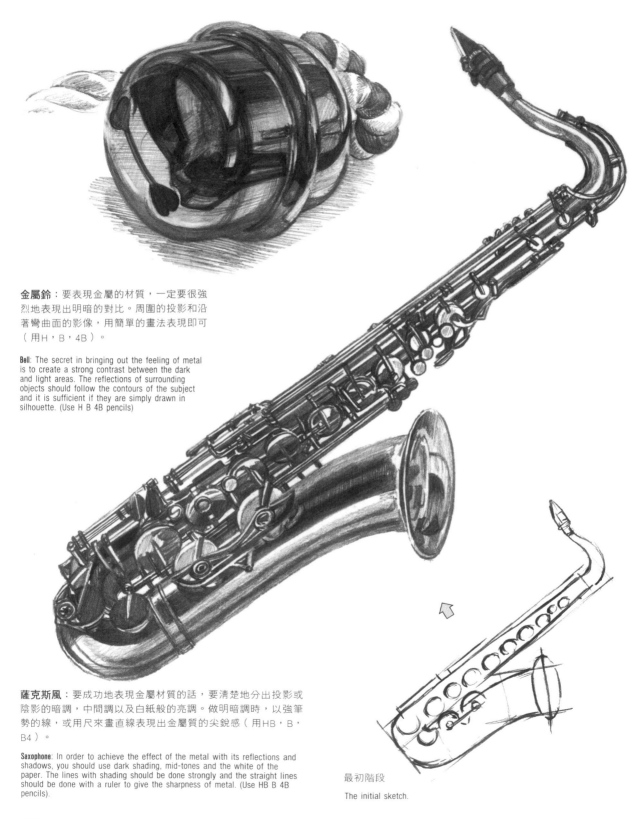

金屬鈴：要表現金屬的材質，一定要很強烈地表現出明暗的對比。周圍的投影和沿著彎曲面的影像，用簡單的畫法表現即可（用H，B，4B）。

Bell: The secret in bringing out the feeling of metal is to create a strong contrast between the dark and light areas. The reflections of surrounding objects should follow the contours of the subject and it is sufficient if they are simply drawn in silhouette. (Use H B 4B pencils)

薩克斯風：要成功地表現金屬材質的話，要清楚地分出投影或陰影的暗調，中間調以及白紙般的亮調。做明暗調時，以強筆勢的線，或用尺來畫直線表現出金屬質的尖銳感（用HB，B，B4）。

Saxophone: In order to achieve the effect of the metal with its reflections and shadows, you should use dark shading, mid-tones and the white of the paper. The lines with shading should be done strongly and the straight lines should be done with a ruler to give the sharpness of metal. (Use HB B 4B pencils).

最初階段

The initial sketch.

桌上的靜物：把斜後方來的光線所造成的明暗關係一起來。省略竹籃中陰暗的網目，這和正面網目的畫法是不一樣的。布上的模樣給予明暗的變化，表現出透明的空間感（用HB，2B）。

Tabletop Still-life: Make sure that the light coming diagonally from behind is the same over the whole picture. The shadowed weaving inside the basket can be simplified whereas the shadowed section on the front of the basket is drawn in detail The variation in light and dark on the pattern of the cloth also help to make it bright, clear picture. (Use HB 2B pencils)

配置與明暗的平衡
The Balance of Contrast and Position

在配置不同顏色，不同質感的物體時，不能只看形態來決定畫面的構圖。鉛筆素描必須要考慮到黑白明暗的平衡。具有亮調、中間調、暗調的物體，在配置的時候，暗的部分重疊，亮的部分重疊，會造成物體的形態和特徵變得曖昧不明，好好利用明暗對比的效果是非常重要的。

When using subjects with different texture, you must not decide on the composition through shape alone. In a monotone, pencil drawing it is necessary to give thought to the balance between light and dark when positioning objects. When you have dark, mid and light tones, make sure that dark objects do not lie next to other dark ones or light objects lie next to other light ones or the shapes will tend to merge. In order to create a good sketch, it is important to try and achieve a good contrast between objects.

從前面往後的配置是亮調、暗調、中間調的順序，即使各個物體重疊，也不會曖昧不明。

Place the objects with light tones in the front followed by dark tones with the mid-tones in the rear. By arranging things in this way, even if they overlap, the shapes do not become confused.

第 4 章
人物素描

Chapter 4
Drawing People

骨　骼
The Skeleton

人物的素描，首先要理解在皮膚表面上顯示出來的骨骼的位置和形態。有動作變化的部份是頭骨、背骨、手足的骨骼等。沒有變化的是頭蓋骨、胸廓、骨盤等。爲了要捕捉動作，先把不會動的部份畫成單純的形狀，再將背骨做成一條延長線。

骨骼：在皮膚表面可以看得出來的用粗線表示。

The skeleton: The parts that show through the skin have been drawn in thick lines.

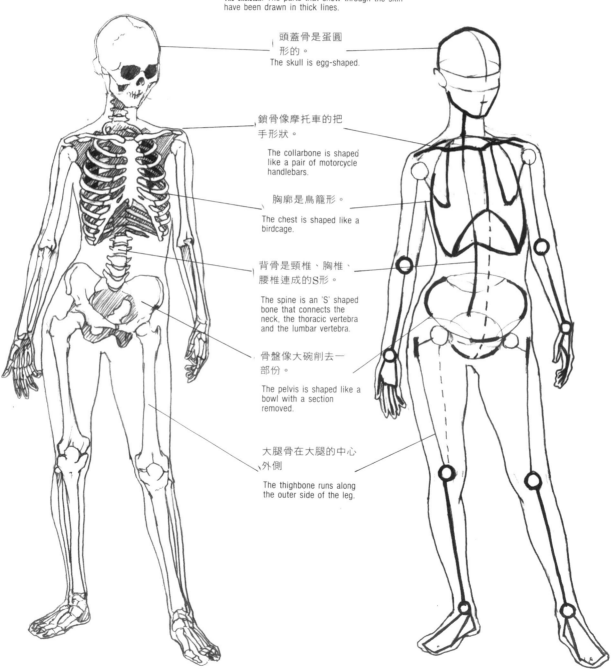

頭蓋骨是蛋圓形的。
The skull is egg-shaped.

鎖骨像摩托車的把手形狀。
The collarbone is shaped like a pair of motorcycle handlebars.

胸廓是鳥籠形。
The chest is shaped like a birdcage.

背骨是頸椎、胸椎、腰椎連成的S形。
The spine is an 'S' shaped bone that connects the neck, the thoracic vertebra and the lumbar vertebra.

骨盤像大碗削去一部份。
The pelvis is shaped like a bowl with a section removed.

大腿骨在大腿的中心外側
The thighbone runs along the outer side of the leg.

When drawing people, it is useful if you understand the construction of the skeleton. The movable parts of the skeleton are; the neck, the spine, and the arms and legs. The immovable parts are skull, the chest and the pelvis. In order to produce a feeling of movement the immovable parts should be simplified and drawn as extensions of the spine.

重心：一般自然的姿勢下，通常重心（體重）都會偏重於一邊的腳。重心放在一邊的腳上，這一邊的肩膀會比其他一邊的肩膀下垂，腰部卻相反地會提高。

The center of gravity: In a natural pose, the bodies weight will center on one of the legs. The shoulder on side of the leg that is carrying the weight will be lower than the other one and the pelvis will slope in the opposite direction.

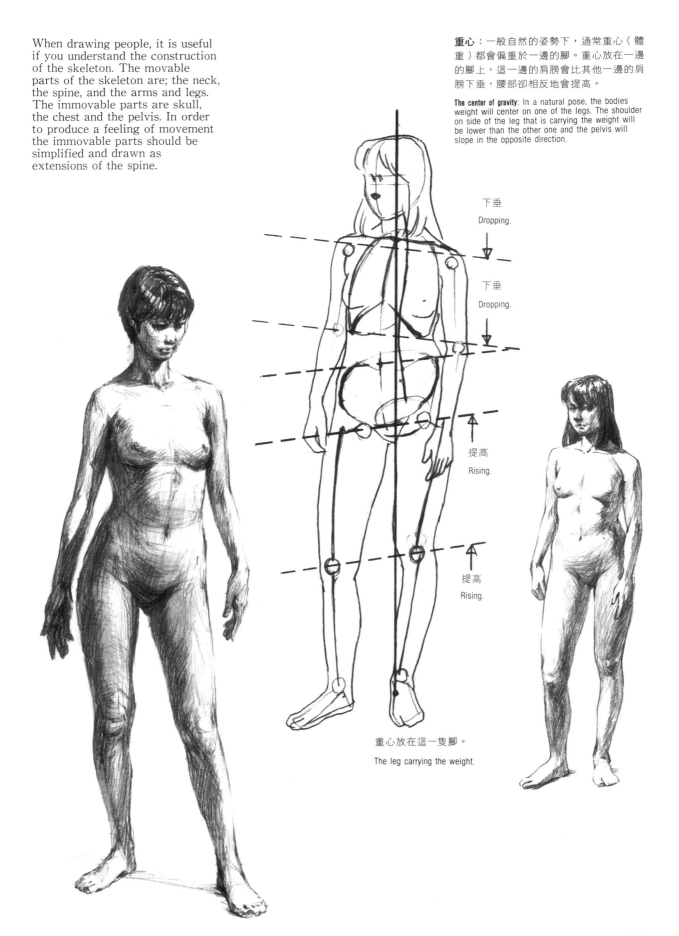

下垂
Dropping.

下垂
Dropping.

提高
Rising.

提高
Rising.

重心放在這一隻腳。

The leg carrying the weight.

形態單純化
Simplifying the Figure

人體在基本上是由立方體和圓柱體組合而成的。以這種觀點來看的話，即使較困難的視點、較複雜的姿勢，也能抓住整體的關聯性以及較深處所應有的形態感，來輕鬆地描繪人體。

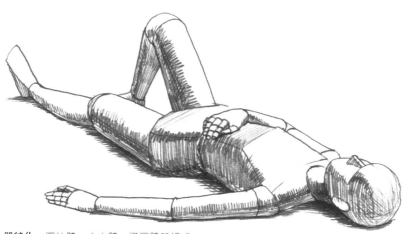

單純化：圓柱體、立方體、蛋圓體所組成的。

Simplification: Cylinders, cubes and an egg-shape combined.

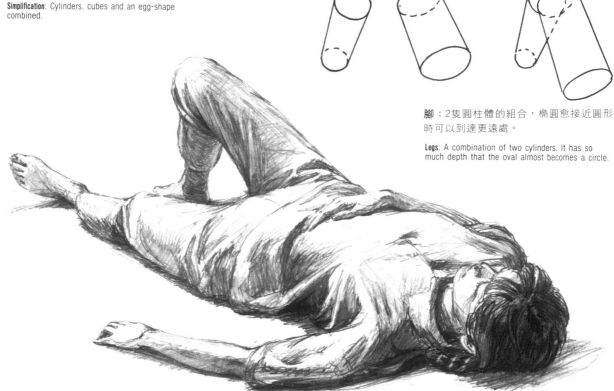

腳：2隻圓柱體的組合，橢圓愈接近圓形時可以到達更遠處。

Legs: A combination of two cylinders. It has so much depth that the oval almost becomes a circle.

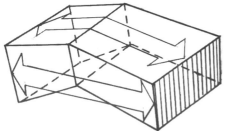

胸和腰：把斜線部份看成肩部，胸部、和腰部看成箱形。箭頭表示各個方向和更遠處。

Chest and waist: The section that will become the shoulders (shaded area), the chest and the hips drawn as cubes. The arrows show the direction and depth.

A human figure is basically a
combination of cubes and
cylinders and if you look at it this
way, a difficult viewpoint or a
complicated pose becomes much
simpler and it is easy to see the
connection between the various
parts.

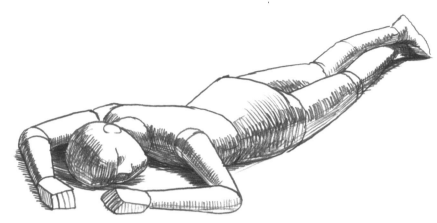

單純化：圓柱體、立方體、蛋圓體的組合。

Simplification: A combination of cylinders, cubes and an egg-shape.

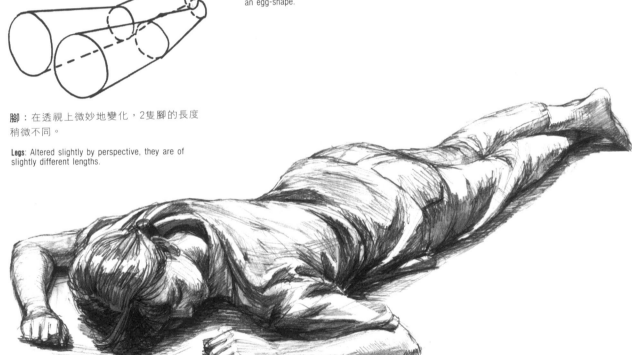

腳：在透視上微妙地變化，2隻腳的長度
稍微不同。

Legs: Altered slightly by perspective, they are of slightly different lengths.

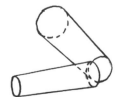 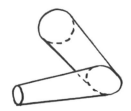

手腕：將圓柱體分解畫出，再接合。

Arms: Draw the cylinders first, then connect them.

全身的比例
Proportion on the Full Figure

青年男子的比率＝4等份・頭部的長度　　A young man's proportions ＝ Divided into Four.

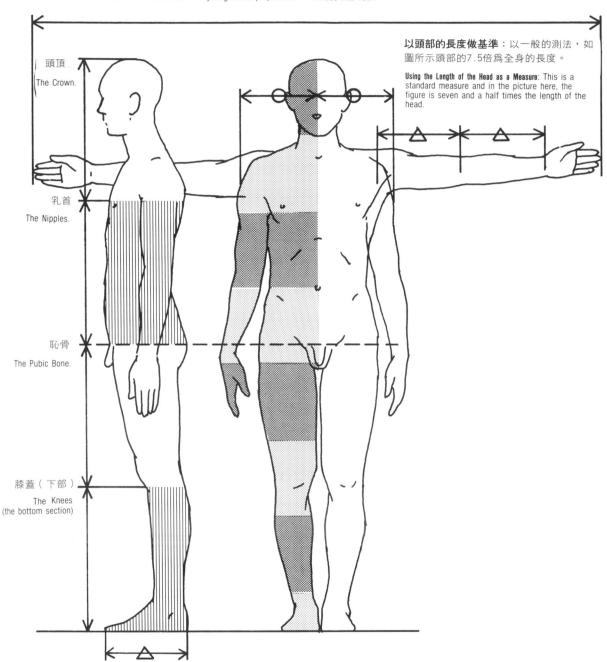

頭頂
The Crown.

乳首
The Nipples.

恥骨
The Pubic Bone.

膝蓋（下部）
The Knees
(the bottom section)

以頭部的長度做基準：以一般的測法，如圖所示頭部的7.5倍為全身的長度。

Using the Length of the Head as a Measure: This is a standard measure and in the picture here, the figure is seven and a half times the length of the head.

全身4等份割：以恥骨為中心，將全身分割為2等份，再以乳首和膝蓋做基準分割成4等份。這樣上面的長度雖比頭部較長，但使用上非常方便。

Dividing the body into four: First split the body into two at the pubic bone then split both sections into two again, one at the nipples, the other at the knee. This is more convenient than using the length of the head as the scale is larger.

量量看各部位的長度：以腳的長度（△）做基準，我們可以發現到上手臂的長度和下手臂的長度也是等長。以頭的長度（○）做基準，雙肩的幅度恰好是2倍。兩手平伸的話恰好和全身等長。

Using different parts of the body as measures, you will see that the length of the foot (△) is equal to the length of the arm from the shoulder to the elbow and from the elbow to the wrist. Equally, if you use the length of the head (○), you will notice that the shoulders are twice its size. If both arms are held out, their length will be equal to the height of the body.

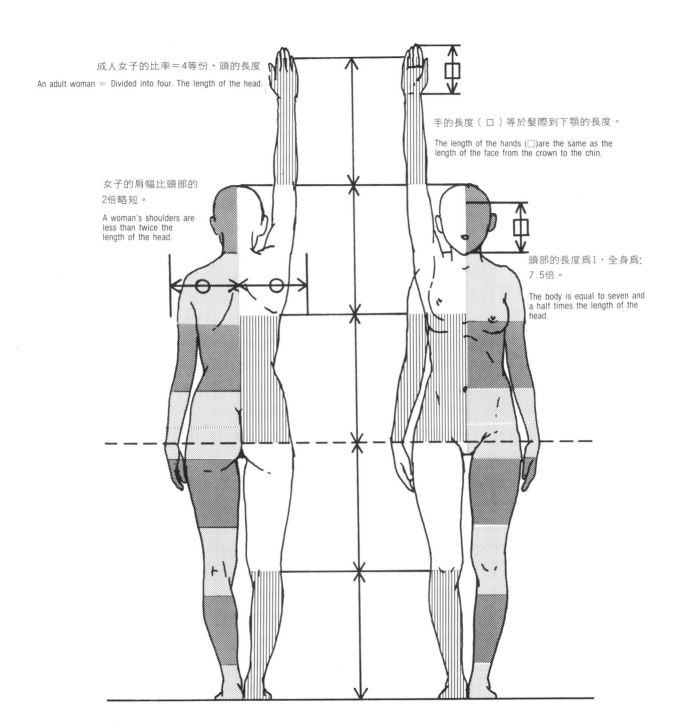

成人女子的比率＝4等份・頭的長度

An adult woman = Divided into four. The length of the head.

手的長度（ 口 ）等於髮際到下顎的長度。

The length of the hands (□)are the same as the length of the face from the crown to the chin.

女子的肩幅比頭部的
2倍略短。

A woman's shoulders are less than twice the length of the head.

頭部的長度為1，全身為:
7.5倍。

The body is equal to seven and a half times the length of the head.

　　在描繪全身時，先將全身分割
，以身體的一個部位代替量尺，求
出各個部位的正確比例。這雖是很
古老的方法，但是非常方便。

When drawing a full-figure, it is useful to break the body down into its components and use one of them as a measure to ensure that you get the proportions correct. This is a very ancient technique, but a useful one to master when drawing people.

衣服的皺褶
Folds in clothes

　　身體雖然被衣服包著，但是肩膀、手肘、膝蓋會突出布料從外觀上顯示出來。這些突出的部位，拉緊的地方清晰地描繪、鬆弛的地方清淡地描繪。還有不要忘記鬆弛布料附近的陰影。

When drawing figures, the shoulders, elbows, knees etc. are often represented through the clothes. The creases formed by these protruding areas should be drawn clearly while hanging folds should be drawn lightly. You must also remember to draw in the shading and shadow formed by hanging folds.

和肩部有關聯的皺褶。

The creases running down from the shoulder.

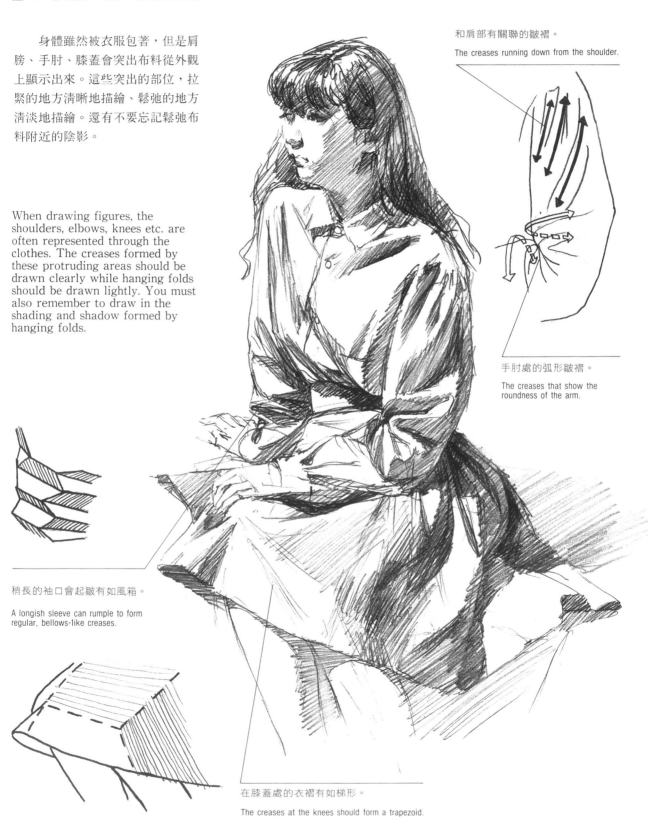

手肘處的弧形皺褶。

The creases that show the roundness of the arm.

稍長的袖口會起皺有如風箱。

A longish sleeve can rumple to form regular, bellows-like creases.

在膝蓋處的衣褶有如梯形。

The creases at the knees should form a trapezoid.

手肘頂點處所拉成的皺褶。

The crease that is pulled by the elbow.

注意裙子下擺皺褶處所隱藏的点
部份。

The folds of the hem. Note the hidden
line of the fold (shown in dotted line).

在腰部束腰時所產生的皺褶。

The creases caused by the
drawing in of the dress at the
waist.

襯衫的陰影部份。

The shading and shadow
of the blouse.

襯衫的影子。

The shading runs down the
blouse.

穿衣服的人物
People Wearing Clothes

最重要的是要透過衣服畫出人
體的存在。雖然姿勢不一樣會有所
不同，因為衣服拉緊，在身體的相
反側人顯得鬆弛，而身體也隱藏在
其中。一般在外觀上突出的部份是
肩、胸、手肘、膝蓋等。

光線在上方所產生黑調子的變化。

The effect of the light from above on the black shading.

亮　　Light.

暗　　Dark.

亮　　Light.

在膝蓋上有裙子的影子。

The skirt throws a shadow
on the knees.

黑棉布的短袖上衣和褲子：筆壓減弱，不要破壞紙質的表面，
可表現出布料的柔軟感（用2B,4B）。

A black, cotton, sleeveless blouse and skirt: Do not apply too much pressure to the
pencil. By leaving the grain of the paper unflattened, it will produce the soft
texture of the material (Use 2B 4B pencils)

裙子上的褶紋是山（明）和谷（暗）的對
應關係。

The pleats of the skirt can be shown by their
peaks (light) and valleys (dark)

It is important to draw the parts of the body that make their presence known through the clothes. Although it changes with the pose, the body will push against the clothes on one side, causing them to stretch while on the other side, the material will be hanging in folds. The most common parts of the body to be seen through the clothes are the shoulders, the bust, elbows, knees and other pointed areas.

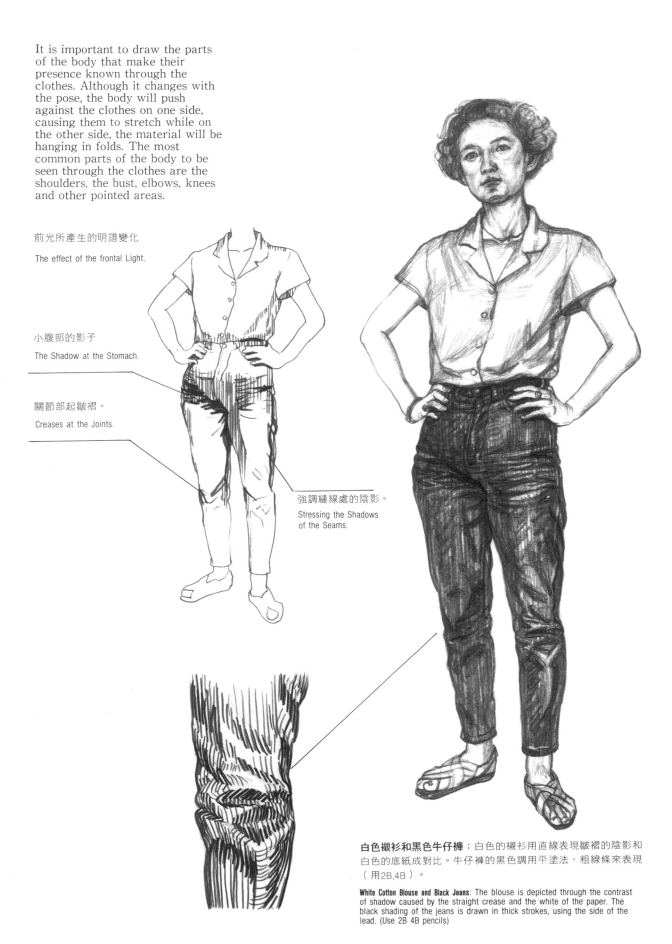

前光所產生的明譜變化
The effect of the frontal Light.

小腹部的影子
The Shadow at the Stomach.

關節部起皺褶。
Creases at the Joints.

強調縫線處的陰影。
Stressing the Shadows of the Seams.

白色襯衫和黑色牛仔褲：白色的襯衫用直線表現皺褶的陰影和白色的底紙成對比。牛仔褲的黑色調用平塗法、粗線條來表現（用2B,4B ）。

White Cotton Blouse and Black Jeans: The blouse is depicted through the contrast of shadow caused by the straight crease and the white of the paper. The black shading of the jeans is drawn in thick strokes, using the side of the lead. (Use 2B 4B pencils)

光線在上方所產生的明暗變化。

The effect of the upper lighting on the shading.

要理解當花格子模樣被皺褶隱藏時的情形。

Make sure you understand what happens to the pattern when it is hidden in a crease.

花格子的套裝: 小心正確地描繪花格子的模樣,尤其是被身體或皺褶所隱藏的地方。隨後再塗上明暗(用HB,4B)。

A Checked Dress: Take care to draw the checked pattern accurately where it is hidden by the body or creases and then fill in the shading. (Use HB 4B pencils)

白色上下套裝：用陰影、頭髮、背景的暗
調子和白紙的白色成明暗的對比，突顯白
色的衣服（用HB,2B）。

White Two-piece: The whiteness of the clothes is
made to stand out through the contrast of the
heavy shading of the shadows, the hair and the
background. (Use HB 2B pencils)

大腿部皺褶的明暗關係：斜線部份是陰暗處。黑色部份是
陰影，箭頭是指皺褶的流向。

The Shading of the Creases on the Legs: The hatched area is shade, the
black area is shadow and the arrows show the direction of the creases.

將主體單純化：用明、中、暗大塊的明暗來表現整體。

The subject has been simplified to show the light, mid and dark
tones of shading.

側光所產生大塊明暗的變化。

The variety in shading caused by the side-lighting.

衣領的形狀。

The shape of the collar.

和服：不要太強調用明暗的對比來表現絹布的柔軟感覺。畫出重要的陰暗部份後，重複且流暢地畫出陰影（用HB、4B）。

Kimono: The softness of the silk is illustrated by not adding much contrast when shading. After the main areas of shade have been drawn, go over the area repeatedly to build up a smooth shading. (Use HB 4B pencils)

從前面所見的袖子形狀。

A sleeve from the front.

在描繪人物時，把圖樣畫得太細膩，會模糊整體的焦點。

When drawing a person, if you fill in the pattern of the clothes in this much detail, it draws attention away from the picture as a whole.

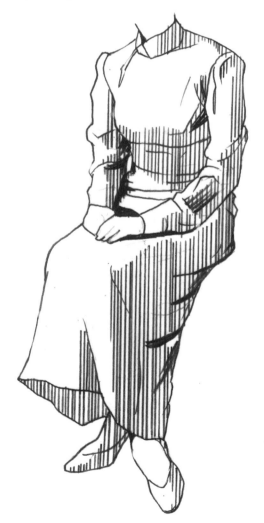

側光所產生大塊明暗的變化。

The heavy shading caused by side lighting.

旗袍：將衣服上的圖樣太細膩地描繪的話，會失去整體的平衡，可作適度的省略。胸部上的圖樣有反光，所以用清淡的描繪，能看出一點點的模樣即可（用HB,4B）。

A China Dress: If the pattern of the dress is drawn in too much detail it will spoil the total balance of the picture so it should be abbreviated as necessary. The pattern on the upper chest is burnt out by the light so only a minimum is necessary. (Use HB 4B pencils.)

頭 部
The Head

要表現頭部的特徵，首先要把握住下顎、臉頰、顏面上等骨骼的形態，然後再抓準眼、鼻、口的位置關係。

依繪畫者的視點不同，臉部各器官的位置關係也會隨著變化。基本上一定要先理解比例關係。

向正面的臉。

Full Face.

側面的臉。

Side View.

正面、側面的頭部比例。從額、眉到鼻的長度等於從鼻到下顎的長度。眼睛的位置恰好在頭頂和下顎的中央，男子在中央略上方，女子略下方。年齡愈小的話，眼睛的位置愈往下。

Proportion of the Full Face and Side View of the Head. The forehead, the distance from the eyebrows to the nose and the distance from the nose to the chin are all approximately the same.
The eyes come approximately halfway between the top of the head and the chin. A man's eyes are slightly above the centerline while a woman's are slightly below. Also, the younger the subject, the lower the eyes are positioned.

In order to bring out the particular characteristics of a face you should first start with the areas where the bones show through the skin such as the chin, cheeks, forehead. Once these have been drawn you can next move on to the eyes, nose and mouth. Depending on the viewpoint of the artist, the relationship between the various parts of the face may alter slightly so it is important to have a firm understanding of the basic proportions.

往上看的臉。

Looking up.

往下看的臉。

Looking down.

往上看時，耳朵的位置在眼、鼻的下方。

When looking up, the ears fall below the eyes and nose.

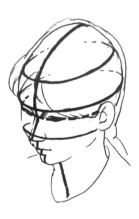

往下看時，耳朵的位置在眼、鼻的上方。

When looking down, the ears fall above the eyes and nose.

男女的頭部
Male and Female Heads

男
Man.

女
Woman.

年青男女：年青的肌膚有彈力有光澤，用較強的筆勢和筆壓來表現明暗。肌膚的調子大都用明亮調，少用中間調，這樣和頭髮、眼睛的暗調成對比，可以強調年青人的朝氣。

Young People: Young people's skin is taut and shiny so use powerful strokes without too much pressure when applying the shading. The shading is often slightly lighter than a mid-tone and the contrast of this with the black of the hair and eyes accentuates the feeling of youth.

老人：老人的特徵是肌肉的鬆弛，眼睛周圍、口部周圍的皺紋非常明顯。還有因為骨骼水分減少，會稍微縮小，皮下脂肪也減少，使骨骼變得更裸露。能抓住這些特徵即可。白髮和膚色的明暗對比要比年青人稍弱。

Old People: The characteristic of old people is the way that their skin sags and the wrinkles that appear around the mouth and eyes. Also, due to a drop in moisture the skull shrinks slightly and with the loss of fat beneath the skin, the bones show through quite clearly. These characteristics should be mastered and it must be remembered that as their hair is grey, there is not nearly so much contrast in the shading as there is in young people.

女
Woman.

男
Man.

手　勢
Hand Movement

手的形狀雖然很複雜，但以手指的關節爲基準，測出各個手指的關係位置，就可畫出有立體感的正確形狀。

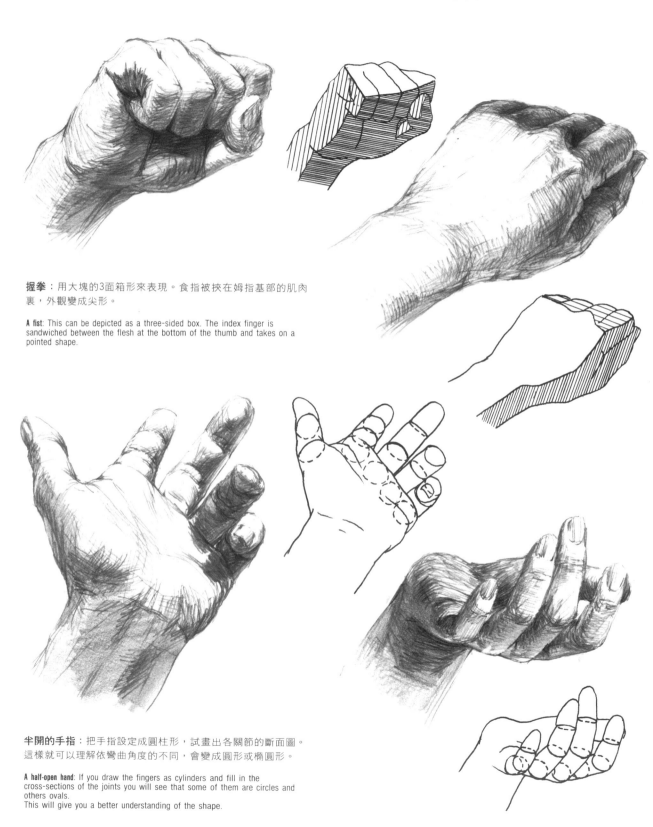

握拳：用大塊的3面箱形來表現。食指被挾在姆指基部的肌肉裏，外觀變成尖形。

A fist: This can be depicted as a three-sided box. The index finger is sandwiched between the flesh at the bottom of the thumb and takes on a pointed shape.

半開的手指：把手指設定成圓柱形，試畫出各關節的斷面圖。這樣就可以理解依彎曲角度的不同，會變成圓形或橢圓形。

A half-open hand: If you draw the fingers as cylinders and fill in the cross-sections of the joints you will see that some of them are circles and others ovals.
This will give you a better understanding of the shape.

Even when the hand is in a
complicated position, if you use
the joints of the fingers as a base
it is possible to work out the
position of each finger and to
produce an accurate
representation with a good feeling
of depth.

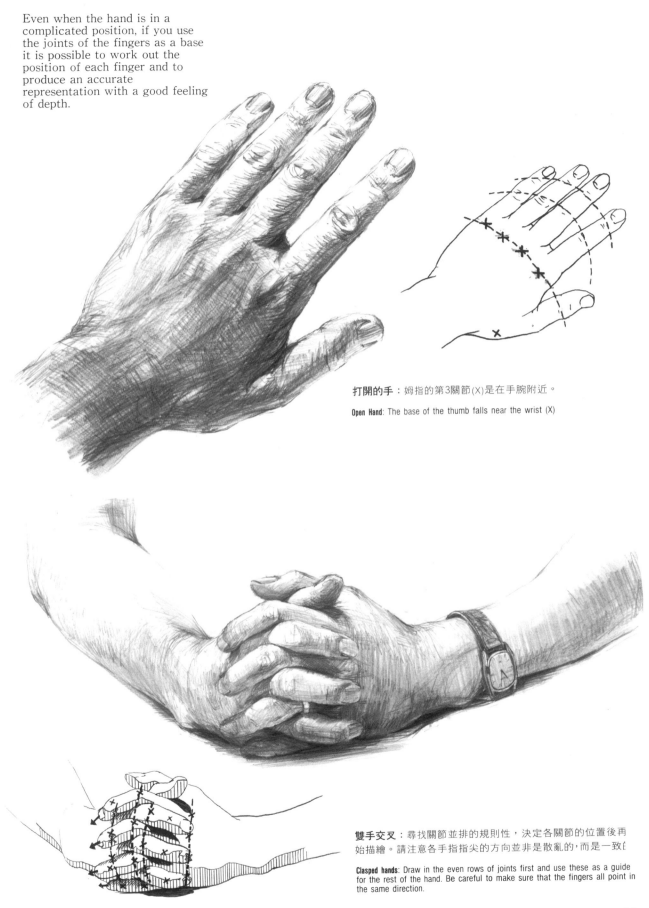

打開的手：姆指的第3關節(X)是在手腕附近。

Open Hand: The base of the thumb falls near the wrist (X)

雙手交叉：尋找關節並排的規則性，決定各關節的位置後再
始描繪。請注意各手指指尖的方向並非是散亂的，而是一致的

Clasped hands: Draw in the even rows of joints first and use these as a guide
for the rest of the hand. Be careful to make sure that the fingers all point in
the same direction.

腳
Feet

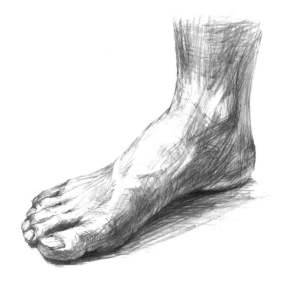

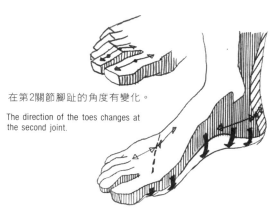

在第2關節腳趾的角度有變化。

The direction of the toes changes at the second joint.

斜線部份是表面的角度，有箭頭的部份是以圓弧的形狀繞入腳底。

The shaded area shows the angle of the surface. The arrows show the parts that curve around to the base.

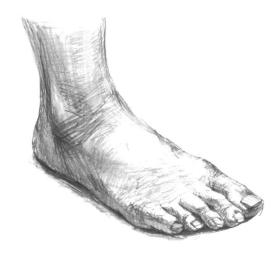

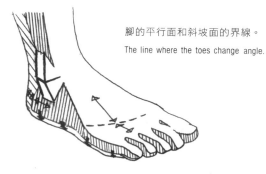

腳的平行面和斜坡面的界線。

The line where the toes change angle.

腳踝用兩面來表現。斜線表示面的角度，箭頭是圓弧形狀繞入腳底。

The ankle is represented by a flat box. The shaded area shows the angle of the surface. The arrows show where the surface curves.

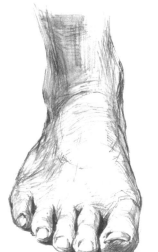

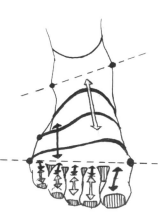

腳踝內側外側的位置關係。

The relative positions of the inner and outer ankles.

足骨：粗線表示形態。→表示腳趾水平面。⇒表示斜面。斜線部份表示垂直面。

Foot bones, the thick lines show the contours. The ➡ shows the horizontal section of the toes. The ⇒ shows the diagonal section. The shaded area shows the vertical section.

第 5 章
風景素描

Chapter 5
Drawing Scenery

空氣透視法
Aerial Perspective

在風景素描時，愈遠的地方愈
明亮，幾乎和天空溶合在一起，變
成一個對比很弱的平板調子。近景
的部分明暗對比愈來愈強，濃淡層
的調階也多。利用這種原理的素描
就是空氣透視法。

When drawing a landscape, tones
lighten with distance, but this
must not be overdone as a picture
where the horizon blends with the
sky becomes flat and
uninteresting. As objects move to
the foreground they have stronger
contrast and the tonal range
increases. This technique is known
as Aerial Perspective.

前面的樹和遠處的樹相比，前面的樹，細
部描繪較深入，明暗對比亦強。

The tree in the front is drawn in more detail than
those to the rear and the contrast is stronger.

遠處的山和近處相比，遠處的山，較明亮
，明暗對比愈來愈弱。

The mountains in the distance are much lighter
than those in the foreground and the contrast is
weaker.

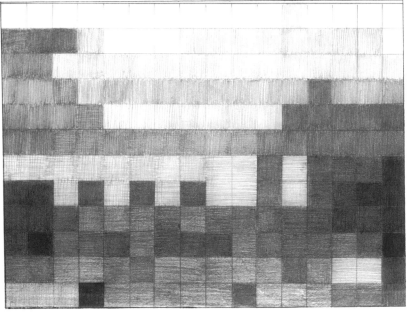

把上圖素描作品的明暗情況代換成下圖的話，可發現愈接近近景，明暗層的調階愈多，
對比也愈強，遠景的話，愈遠愈平板。

When this picture is represented by a tonal pattern it is easy to see how much stronger the contrast is in
the foreground and how it becomes rather flat in the distance.

天空和雲的表現
Expressing the Sky and Clouds

在天空的明暗畫法中，不要忘記以雲的白色來作對比的方法。天空的明暗法和空氣透視法一樣，眼前的物體較濃，遠處的物體較淡，用這樣來表達遠近感。有一種是把天空和雲當背景，襯托出畫面全體。另外一種是把雲畫得非常清淡或者不畫，使畫面的主題突出。

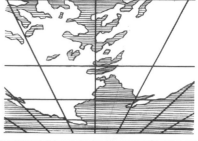

雲的深處
The depth of the clouds.

The sky can be shaded and the white of the paper left to represent the clouds. As with landscapes, aerial perspective should be used, the sky gradually becoming lighter as it moves into the distance. The sky and clouds can be used in the background as a section of the landscape or the clouds can be simplified or even omitted and the sky used to make the main subject stand out.

魚鱗狀的雲，雲和雲之間的距離要縮小，從近處一直往遠方去，好像整體的雲平貼在一塊平面上的感覺，用4B）。

The intervals between the bands of cloud should decrease as it moves into the distance and the whole mass of cloud should be drawn as a single plane. (Use 4B pencil)

天空的明暗使用長尺，以線條的粗密來表現。愈接近地平線天空愈明亮。眼前的雲對比很強烈，遠處的雲較平順（用4B）。

A ruler can be used to shade the sky with the interval between the lines widening towards the horizon. The clouds in the foreground have strong contrast, but those in the back are much flatter. (Use a 4B pencil)

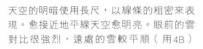

平靜的天空：用鉛筆在砂紙上磨成鉛筆的粉粒狀，放在天空的位置，然後再用面紙和紙筆擦拭，作出明暗的調子。白雲的話用軟橡皮擦處理，最後再用鉛筆來修飾明暗（用4B）。

A mackerel sky : In order to get smooth tone for the sky, rub a pencil against some sandpaper, letting the graphite fall on the section that will become the sky, then use tissue paper and a tortillon to rub it into the paper. The clouds can be lifted out afterwards, using a soft rubber eraser and then the shading added again with a pencil. (Use 4B pencil)

樹木的表現
How to Draw Trees

要表現繁盛的枝葉，先要確定從主幹分出來的支幹方向，隨後不要被一大片的綠色所迷惑，把握住大塊的明暗表現即可，這是最基本的方法。大塊明暗的前後關係，是以光的方向來意識到陰暗的部位，再加以強調。還有葉的特徵，可以描出一部分的葉子，或用軟橡皮擦來處理光亮的部分。

In order to portray the feeling of the foliage, watch how the branches leave the trunk of the tree and do not be confused by the colors but try and grasp the overall shape as a single mass. In order to give depth to the mass, watch the direction of the light and stress the shadows in the shading. The shape of the leaves can be shown to provide interest and highlights can be picked out with a soft rubber eraser.

茂盛的闊葉樹：用大塊如雲般的明暗法。

A broad tree with the foliage drawn in a large mass like a cloud.

樹木的重疊以明暗極大的差別來表現。

A street of trees where the difference between light and shade has been taken to extreme.

針葉樹的特徵：葉形用明暗法，再以軟橡皮擦來調整明暗調子，表現出前後的感覺。

The characteristic shape of the conifer has been expressed with shading then a soft rubber eraser used to add a feeling of depth.

在眼前葉子的形態用軟橡皮擦處理，較深
處的葉子用簡單的輪廓明暗即可。能畫出
樹幹或分枝上的影子的話，更具真實感。

The leaves of the tree in the foreground have been
lifted out with a soft rubber eraser while those in
the distance have been shaded to form silhouettes.
The shadow falling of the trunks and branches
produces a feeling of reality.

建築物的質感
The Texture of Buildings

像建築物那麼大的主體，這和在室內作靜物素描或人物素描，是不同的。因為建築物中有各種不同的材質，其表現方法也不一樣。在大場面的情況，不要拘泥於小節，用大塊的亮面、中間調、陰影3階段來描繪即可。至於材質的特徵，用部分性的描繪，在感覺上質感表現是必要的。在近處的細部描繪和遠處的廣大場面時，雖然都是在同一畫面上，其表現的方法是不同的。

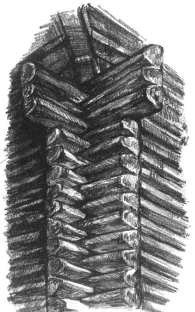

石牆：受光面的石牆形狀用明暗對比來表現。強調陰暗面和光亮面的交界處，其他可省略（用2B）。

Stone Walls : The area that faces the light should be drawn in strong blacks and whites. The area of shadow should be stressed where it meets the light area but the rest can be done roughly. (Use 2B pencil)

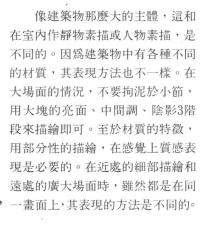

木造的建築物：將木板的特徵部分省略掉（用2B）。

Wooden Building : The best results are achieved if portions of the plank's detail is omitted. (Use 2B pencil)

接近物體畫出質感（用4B）。

Close-up of Textures. (Use 4B pencil)

石牆：確認光線的來源，用黑色調來強調一個一個的石塊形狀，再強調凹凸部分的明亮處，使它更突出。

Stone wall : Decide on the direction of the light and draw each stone separately with strong tones. Exaggerate the roughness of the stones by adding highlights to the high points.

木造的建築物：不必太拘泥於質感，順著木材的形態，給與大塊的明暗即可。（用2B）。

Wooden Building : Do not worry too much about the texture, concentrate on the shape of the wood and add rough toning. (Use 2B pencil)

The texture of a large subject like a building has to be grasped in a different way to small subjects like still-life or portraits. When faced with a large area, do not spend too much time on the intricate details, rather concentrate of the three main sections, highlights, mid-tones and shade and stress the special characteristics of the textures to bring out the feeling of the subject. It should also be borne in mind that a detailed close-up and distant view of the same area should be expressed differently.

大樓的玻璃窗：把全體看成整面的玻璃。玻璃上的建築物的投影，用簡單的剪影法來表現。將天空弄亮，產生畫面上的明暗對比。最後是窗子的框架用軟橡皮橡處理（用4B，2B）。

Glass Windows in a Building : Draw the windows as if they were all one. Draw in the silhouette of buildings reflected in the glass and leave the sky bright, to provide a good contrast. The window frames can be added later, using a soft eraser. (Use 4B, 2B pencils)

紅磚：同樣形狀的集合體，用明暗度的差別來表現。在各塊的接合處，用強力清晰的筆法描繪。

Bricks : They are all the same shape but are differentiated between by varying in tone. Draw the edges where they join clearly.

大理石：大理石的模樣用暈擦的筆法，接合處用直線表現。這樣就可感覺平面上有模樣。

Marble : The pattern is produced by blurring the pencil lines with a tortillon. Once this has been done, draw in the straight lines to illustrate that the pattern is on a flat surface.

混凝土：在平面上幾乎沒有明暗的變化。以中間調全面擦畫後，再加上少許的細部筆法，使它有點變化。

Concrete : Having a flat surface, there is very little variety in tone. Rub in mid-tone and then draw in the details on top to add variety.

透視圖法
Perspective Projection

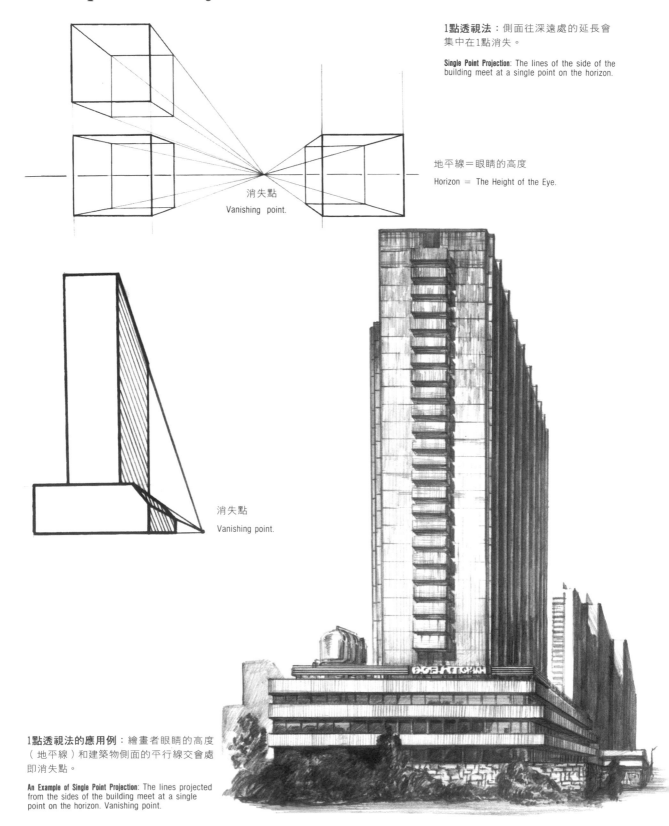

1點透視法：側面往深遠處的延長會集中在1點消失。

Single Point Projection: The lines of the side of the building meet at a single point on the horizon.

地平線＝眼睛的高度

Horizon ＝ The Height of the Eye.

消失點
Vanishing point.

消失點
Vanishing point.

1點透視法的應用例：繪畫者眼睛的高度（地平線）和建築物側面的平行線交會處即消失點。

An Example of Single Point Projection: The lines projected from the sides of the building meet at a single point on the horizon. Vanishing point.

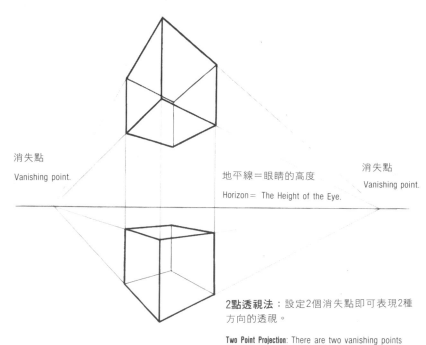

消失點
Vanishing point.

地平線＝眼睛的高度
Horizon＝ The Height of the Eye.

消失點
Vanishing point.

以眼睛的高度和地平線是等高的原理，以及建築物往遠處望去它的延長線和地平線交會於1點的原理，兩者互相應用，用這種透視圖的方法可以描繪出有遠近感的建築物。在地平線交會的點我們稱它爲消失點。在繪畫時我們先想定消失點，可用這原理將建築物一直往遠處表現出來。

The basic rule of perspective states that the horizon should be at the same height as the artist's eye and that the lines showing the depth of the building should meet at a single point on the horizon that is known as the vanishing point. In order to achieve this, it is useful to simplify buildings into simple geometrical shapes and extend the lines back to the vanishing point.

2點透視法：設定2個消失點即可表現2種方向的透視。

Two Point Projection: There are two vanishing points so depth is shown in two directions.

消失點
Vanishing point.

消失點
Vanishing point.

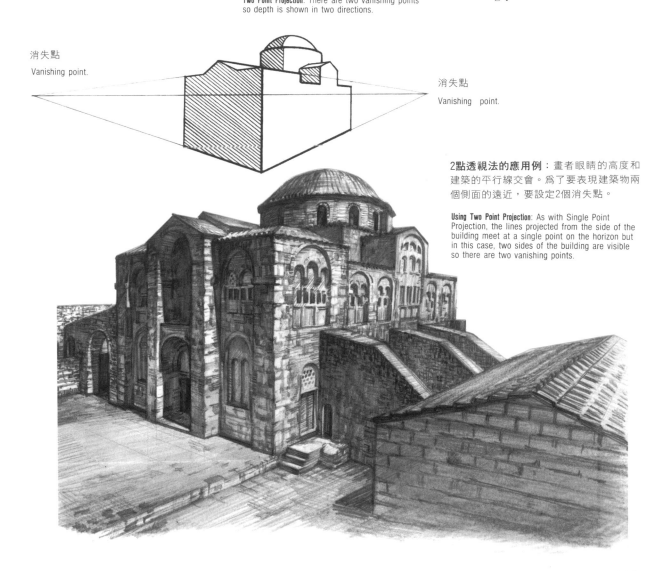

2點透視法的應用例：畫者眼睛的高度和建築的平行線交會。爲了要表現建築物兩個側面的遠近，要設定2個消失點。

Using Two Point Projection: As with Single Point Projection, the lines projected from the side of the building meet at a single point on the horizon but in this case, two sides of the building are visible so there are two vanishing points.

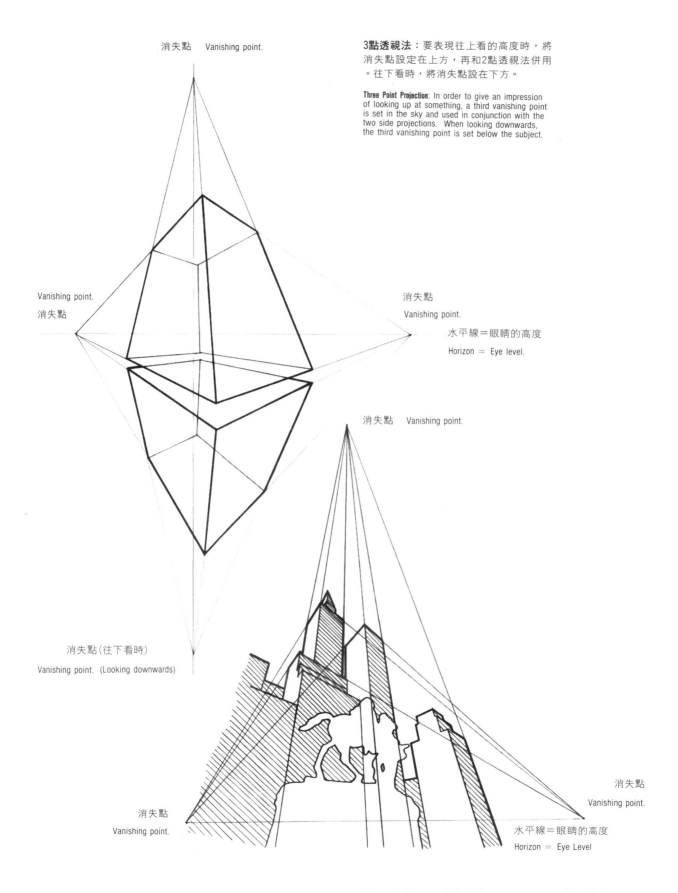

消失點　Vanishing point.

3點透視法：要表現往上看的高度時，將
消失點設定在上方，再和2點透視法併用
。往下看時，將消失點設在下方。

Three Point Projection: In order to give an impression
of looking up at something, a third vanishing point
is set in the sky and used in conjunction with the
two side projections. When looking downwards,
the third vanishing point is set below the subject.

Vanishing point.
消失點

消失點
Vanishing point.

水平線＝眼睛的高度
Horizon ＝ Eye level.

消失點　Vanishing point.

消失點(往下看時)
Vanishing point. (Looking downwards)

消失點
Vanishing point.

消失點
Vanishing point.

消失點
Vanishing point.

水平線＝眼睛的高度
Horizon ＝ Eye Level

3點透視法的應用例：除了2點透視法外，要強調高度時，可在
上方任意設定消失點。

An Example of Three Point Projection: In addition to the two side projections, a
third vanishing point has been set in the sky to increase the impression of
height.

建築物
Buildings

　要畫建築物時，儘可能將建築物的整體，看成一個很單純的形態，這樣就容易畫了。為了要畫出在大地上建築物起來的安定感，即使看不見地面，也要以想定的地面和透視法來設定消失點。

You will find it much easier to draw buildings if you simplify them and concentrate on the overall shape. In order to create an impression of solidity, it is useful to project the sides down to the ground, even if it is hidden in the final picture and to check the perspective too.

高樓前面的通路是立方體的組合。

The passageway in front of the building is a combination of cubes.

以基本形態（立方體）來理解橋的構造。

It is important to have a good grasp of the actual shape of the bridge as a whole.

面向橋墩，要確實地描繪水面（如地面）、橋、岸邊的話，用1點透視法設定消失點即可。

The surface of the river and the sections of the bridge should be projected to the vanishing point to check perspective.

106

注意圓球體的支柱和地面的接觸點，支柱
的影子是順著圓球體而形成圓弧狀。

Check the position of the pillars supporting the
tank. The shadows of the pillars will be curved
where they wrap themselves around the tank.

圓球支柱和地面的關係。

The position of the pillars and the ground.

這是立方體與圓柱體組合而成的2點透視。

The Two Point Projection of the combination of two
cylinders and a rectangle.

在大樓的圓弧面上有效地表現突出的亮部
，可表現大樓圓形部分的結構。

The highlight on the curved end of this building
was used effectively to show the roundness of the
construction.

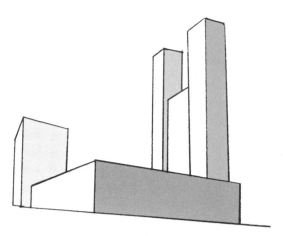

把立方體的組合當做基本型態。

The basic shape is a collection of rectangles.

建築中的高樓：雖然是複雜的對象，但是基本上可以用立方體的組合來理解它的結構。要表現它的高度，以右側的高樓使用3點透視法描繪。要表現空間的寬廣，在前面使用陰暗調，強調樓角的明暗對比。陰暗的調子愈往遠處愈明亮，明暗的對比也愈弱（用2H，HB，3B）。

A Building Under Construction: This is a very complicated subject, but it can be broken down into a combination of rectangles. In order to give a feeling of height, the tower building on the right used three point projection. As it covers such a large area, the shadows in the foreground were drawn very dark and contrast given on the corners while the shading in the rear was much lighter and the contrast became much weaker. (Use 2H HB 3B pencils)

鐵塔：要正確地描繪我們正在仰望的鐵塔，必須把握住挾在4支鐵柱間的水平面（如左圖），注意從底部一直往上去，這些平面都有變化。愈往上去，形狀愈寬廣，等距的間隔也愈來愈窄，先決定最下層，正中間層，最上層的平面即可。

A Steel Tower: When looking up at a tower like this, it is important that the rate of distortion of the horizontal lines between the four main supports should be carried out accurately. As the tower moves to the top, the bottom of the horizontal girders will seem to grow broader and the interval between them narrower. It is useful if you draw in a square platform at the base, one in the middle and one at the top to act as guides.

往上仰望時底部的形狀。

The shape of the platforms when seen from below.

寺塔：把它看做由立方體重疊起來的建築物。屋頂底面的平面和其高度的位置，和鐵塔的注意要點一樣。寺塔屋頂所特有的斜弧，把它看做內接在立方體內的物體。

A Pagoda: This building consists of several rectangles set on top of each other. The way that the underside of the roofs can be seen and the way in which the shape distorts makes it similar to a steel tower. The typical temple roof shape can be mastered quite easily if you treat it as a cube and then cut away the unnecessary sections afterwards..

屋頂的形狀用1點透視法當做內接在立方體內。

To draw the roof, start with a polygon that has been corrected for perspective using a single point projection.

整面玻璃的大樓：投映在玻璃上的藍天和白雲，用2種明暗度來表現，在某些圓形的玻璃上加上不同明暗的變化，畫出整棟的大樓。在描畫整體的形狀時，用2點透視法的原則，在2邊側面的玻璃窗框的角度，由上而下一直變化下來即可（用HB，4B）。

Glass-fronted Buildings: The reflections of the sky and the clouds were drawn in two tones but the reflection in all the windows is not the same and this distortion of the glass helps to give a feeling of scale to the subject. It should be remembered that as this subject was drawn using two point projection, the angle of the window frames changes from top to bottom. (Use HB 4B pencils)

體育館：爲了要畫出橫向發展的建築物的一些變化，將地面畫
寬闊一點，將消失點設定在右側的遠方，畫面上要畫出往深遠
處的感覺。

Stadium: In order to give some variety to this wide building, a vanishing point
was set to the rear right and single point projection used to give a feeling of
depth.

水的質感
Water Texture

水會因為光的反射和投影而有所變化，積極地利用這種特徵來表現即可。在海上或河川上的水面有規則性、重覆性的波浪，我們要找出波浪起伏的形態，尤其是明部和暗部的互動關係是非常的重要。筆觸沿著波浪的起伏重疊畫出，並且要表現出流動的感覺。

畫風景中的水面時，要確實地把握住光的影響，利用空氣透視法表現出近遠刻度似的情景是最基本的技法。

In order to depict water, it must be remembered that it is nothing but an interplay of light and reflection. The sea or rivers are formed of a regular repetition of waves and attention must be paid to the areas of light and shade. Building up the shading along the lines of the waves allows you to produce a feeling of flowing movement.
Water is used in landscapes to accentuate the relationship of light and dark and to provide a feeling of depth and scale.

微波：省略掉遠處的波紋，愈接近近處，陰影的明暗調階愈多（用4B）。

Ripples: The waves are drawn roughly in the distance, but with more contrast as they move into the foreground. (use 4B pencil)

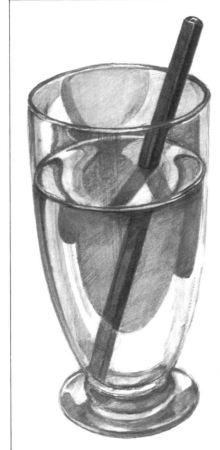

水滴

A drop of the water.

杯中的水平面：要描繪水的話，最重要的要素是反射和投影，用棒插入水中可表現出透明感。

An example of water in a glass: Water is depicted by reflection and refraction. The stick in the glass helps to stress the transparency of the water.

114

逆光的海: 在畫面中央,波浪明暗分界處,用重點式的描繪,
最後在最亮處用軟橡皮擦處理(用4B)。

A Backlit sea: Most care should be taken over the waves in the middle of the picture where light and dark meet. The highlights can be added later using a soft rubber eraser.　(use 4B pencil)

逆光的海浪: 好像連綿的大小山巒,用明部和暗部對比的手法
(用4B)。

Backlit Waves: A repeating pattern of large and small peaks. Care must be taken over the contrast of light and shade. (use 4B pencil)

河川和橋：從正面看，整個橫跨的橋是左右對稱的，橋的形狀却缺乏變化，但是只要把視點稍微移動，就可以看到橋墩和鐵架。

水面和橋用1點透視法，一直表現到遠處。中央是橋，前面2分之1是水面，構圖上並不富於變化。所以把天空明亮的反射調表現在波浪上，以及誘導視線從近處的波浪往橋的方向移動，這樣就可以補救這單調的畫面（用AB，2B，4B）。

River and Bridge: A bridge looked at straight on is very balanced and lacking in interest, but by changing your viewpoint only a little the beams and girders take on a completely different appearance. A One Point Projection has been used for both the bridge and river, but with the bridge in the center and the bottom half of the picture taken up by water, the subject was lacking in variety. In order to compensate for this, a light sky was added and reflected in the water. The light on the waves in the river serves to draw the eyes towards the bridge and saves the picture from becoming too monotonous. (Use HB 2B 4B Pencils)

要以黑白的對比當做畫面的構成，追求紙和塑料的質感。　學生作品例（用3H，H，2B，6B）。

A design by students that stresses the contrast of black and white and 1 the textures of plastic and paper. (Use 3H H 2B 6B pencils)

後記　　　　　　　　　　*Postscript*

　　如果你已經熟練素描的基本表現和技法的話，下一個步驟就是希望你嘗試用自己獨特的方法來表現。例如，你可以忽視物體原來的顏色或立體感，只追求物體的質感，或者是故意去誇張物體的比例，這是一件非常有趣的事。但是不要忘記一定要熟練基本的技法。不只這樣，你還要具有向新的東西挑戰的精神，發現自己特有的個性盡情地表現。

After you have mastered the basic techniques of pencil drawing, the next step is to discover your own method of expression. For instance, you could ignore the subjects local color or feeling of depth and concentrate solely on its texture or even purposely distort it. It is important to master the basic techniques first but you should not let it end there, you should be willing to try something new and discover your own personal style.

　　本書中文譯本是依日文原文的翻譯，和英譯的文章稍微有點出入，但原義與精神是一致不變的。稍有誤差的地方敬請讀者見諒及指教。

東京武藏野美術學院・製作成員
TOKYO MUSASHINO ACADEMY OF ART

監　　　修　山内英雄
Edited　　by　HIDEO YAMAUCHI
執　　　筆　大熊弘文
Written　by　HIROFUMI OHKUMA
作　品　例　三澤寛志
Examples　by　HIROSHI MISAWA
　　　　　　P.25,28,29,31,32,33,34,35,38,39,69,72,73,74,75,76,
　　　　　　77,78,79,83,86,87,88,89,90,91,92,98,99
　　　　　　高沢哲明
　　　　　　TETSUAKI TAKAZAWA
　　　　　　P.42,43,46,47,60,62,63,64,65,66,67,68
　　　　　　高橋新三郎
　　　　　　SHINZABURO TAKAHASHI
　　　　　　P.20,48,49,52,53,54,55,56,58,59,70,94,95,115
　　　　　　石原　崇
　　　　　　TAKASHI ISHIHARA
　　　　　　P.11,12,13,14,15,16,17,36,37,44,45,97,100,101,102,
　　　　　　103,104,105,106,114
　　　　　　大寺　聡
　　　　　　SATOSHI OHTERA
　　　　　　P.6,7,10,18,19,22,23,24,26,27,28,29,30,40,41,50,114
　　　　　　大熊弘文
　　　　　　HIROFUMI OHKUMA
　　　　　　P.80,81,82,84,85,96,102,103,108,109,110,111,112,
　　　　　　113,115,116,117

英　文　翻　譯　Gavin Frew
版　面　設　計　株式会社エイジ